RING LARDNER'S
YOU KNOW ME AL

RING LARDNER'S YOU KNOW ME AL

The Comic Strip Adventures of Jack Keefe

With Preface by Al Capp

A Harvest Book
Harcourt Brace Jovanovich/Bruccoli Clark
New York and London

Printed in the United States of America

Library of Congress Cataloging in Publication Data

Lardner, Ring Wilmer, 1885–1933
Ring Lardner's You know me Al.

(A Harvest book)
Cartoons by Will B. Johnstone and Dick Dorgan.
I. Johnstone, Will B.   II. Dorgan, Dick.
III. Title.   IV. Title: You know me Al.
PN6727.L3Y6   741.5′973   78-20641
ISBN 0-15-676696-5

First edition

A   B   C   D   E   F   G   H   I   J

HBJ

Contents

Preface

by Al Capp

I reread Ring Lardner every few years. I love him still, yet in the last decades he has moved from being a mirror of Americans to being a reminder that there once were Americans like those he wrote about. Jack Keefe, the baseball pitcher in "You Know Me Al," no longer exists. He was a simple man. He pitched the best he could; he took what they paid him; he had no say over where he worked; he worked wherever the owners traded him.

He had no philosophy, but he knew a few truths. "That's the hell of it, in baseball," he wrote to Al; "it costs too much to take your wife on a trip with you, and it ain't safe to leave them at home." He enjoyed his years at the top, or as close as he could get to it. He didn't save much during those years, because, generally, he wasn't paid much. Since he acted like a big star, everybody expected him to pick up the checks, and when he had no choice he did—reluctantly. He was easy to understand and to laugh at. He was considered a lucky guy to marry a girl as gorgeous as Edna. She was a cretin like him, but this was considered trifling in a girl with her looks. They spoke a simple, direct, young-married-folks' dialog. He made everything he'd done, everything he dreamed of doing, seem bigger. Edna's acidity made it all seem less. Was I the only reader who regarded her as a pest, and Jack Keefe as a doomed hero, always reaching for the sky, never making it, but forever trying?

If Ring Lardner were alive today, I wonder whether he could have created Jack Keefe. Lardner's sympathy was always with the underdog, but underdogs are harder to sympathize with in today's game.

It is increasingly difficult to see players making six-figure salaries, who have stock options and foreign bank accounts, as ordinary guys with ordinary aspirations. Baseball players today are so smart I don't think Lardner would have touched them. And so, let us be grateful that Lardner lived while Jack Keefe was possible.

A word about Dick Dorgan. As a kid, I had come to New York from Boston, with an armful of cartoons, one an imitation of the late, great Tad Dorgan. At the Associated Press an editor looked at them and said, "One hour ago Dick Dorgan resigned from a cartoon he was doing for us. Would you take a crack at it for fifty dollars a week?"

And so I spent my first months in New York imitating Dick Dorgan, who imitated his brother Tad. But did he? He had the same perception, but he wasn't as broad. Was he more subtle? Or couldn't he draw at all? Would a broader comic style have given Lardner's dialog a sharper edge? Or did it need that edge? I don't know. Yet that collaboration was a beginning that might have revolutionized the comic strip. A great humorist and a popular artist, combined in a daily column that paid more, if it was popular, than a dozen best-sellers. Nearly forty years ago I tried it by luring the great illustrator Raeburn Van Buren to comics. I wrote one called "Abbie an' Slats." It went well enough for me to try a half-dozen authors. They all thought about it for a week or so, and then they all said they didn't think it was right for them. "Abbie an' Slats" went on for decades, under my authorship, and then under my brother Eliot's. I have always wondered if those authors decided the comic strip wasn't right for them, or if they weren't up to it. Except for Ring Lardner.

Introduction

In September 1922, when the Bell Syndicate began circulating Ring Lardner's comic strip "You Know Me Al," Lardner's naive, letter-writing busher was well-known to American readers. Jack Keefe first appeared in *The Saturday Evening Post* in March 1914. Over the next five years he was the persona of twenty-two other stories which followed his life from his arrival in Chicago as a White Sox pitcher through his experiences in Europe during World War I, as he told it in letters to Al Blanchard, his friend back home in Bedford, Indiana.

The sensitive, knowing satire of these stories is complemented by the expert's knowledge of baseball Lardner brought to his work. The busher stories were set in the real world of baseball among the real men Lardner wrote about in the sports pages of Chicago newspapers. The time was the present, and Keefe's letters dwelled on his day-to-day activities.

Lardner attempted in 1922 to bring that same insider's view of baseball to the comic strip. The strip begins where the stories did—with Keefe reporting to the Chicago White Sox to start his first big-league season—but the plot similarity ends there. The comic strip is set in the twenties, and the fictional characters move among the baseball players of that time.

Lardner expected of his readers a knowledge of contemporary baseball; indeed, "You Know Me Al" ran on the sports page in many papers. Lardner's readers knew that in 1921 Babe Ruth hit fifty-nine home runs; George Sisler stole thirty-five bases; Walter Johnson led the American League in strikeouts; and Detroit led the American League in hitting. The New York Giants were the best team in baseball, followed closely by the New York Yankees; the Chicago White Sox, Keefe's team, were among the worst.

The White Sox were a decimated team in 1922. Three years earlier they had been widely considered a sure bet to win the world championship. Then came the 1919 World Series when the White Sox were nicknamed the "Black Sox" by sports reporters. Eight star players of the White Sox took bribes to throw that series, and in 1920 they were suspended from baseball for life. In 1921 the White Sox finished last in their league. Since two of the men suspended were pitchers, the White Sox were forced to recruit bushers like Keefe.

Nineteen twenty-two was a bad year for pitchers. To revive the attendance which had fallen off after the 1919 scandal, rules were changed to make baseball a hitter's game. The ball was altered to make it livelier, the distance between the pitcher's mound and home plate was reduced, and "unusual pitches," such as the spitball, were outlawed by degrees. Keefe's record in 1922 was 10–8; not bad for a rookie the year both George Sisler and Ty Cobb had season batting averages of over .400 and even the legendary Walter Johnson had 15 wins against 16 losses.

Charles A. Comiskey, owner of the White Sox, was notoriously thrifty. The men on his team in 1919 made between $2,500 and $5,000; only one player, Eddie Collins, commanded as much as $14,500. Keefe's salary of $2,500 was what a busher could have ex-pected from Comiskey in 1922, and while it may have been less than he could have made on another team, money went further in those days when the annual per capita income was less than $700.

But as in all things apart from the pitcher's mound, Keefe was ignorant about money. He—and his wife—spent foolishly, largely to impress others, and Lardner gives an exact accounting of where it all went.

Lardner knew baseball players well. He covered their activities for eight years as a sports reporter and for another six years as a sports columnist. By the early twenties, however, his interests were elsewhere. He was writing a weekly syndicated column, covering special events for the Bell Syndicate, writing sketches for various stage revues, and turning out magazine pieces at the rate of one a month. By the winter of 1924 the comic strip had become a burden, even though it was earning him some $30,000 a year. In January 1925 Lardner quit the strip. His name continued to appear on it until September 1925, but it is clear that he had worked ahead very little and after the first of February the ideas are someone else's.

Lardner wrote continuity for some 700 strips. Of those, 292 have been selected here. We are grateful to the San Francisco Academy of Comic Art, directed by Bill Blackbeard, and to Captain William Loughman, who trimmed "You Know Me Al" from discarded copies of the *Milwaukee Journal,* for their assistance.

—Richard Layman

NOTE: *The headings on the strips are inconsistent because the strips reproduced here—though mostly from the* Milwaukee Journal—*were assembled from several newspapers. Since these strips are reproduced from 55-year-old newspapers, they vary in quality.*

The Busher Comes to Chi

The Busher Settles In

YOU KNOW ME AL　　　　　　　　　　　　　　　　　　　—By RING LARDNER

Learning Signals Wouldn't Strain Him in That Position

He'll Make the "Shrubs" Look Like Poison Ivy

What a Guy Will Do for Love

A Tight Suit for a Tight Guy

YOU KNOW ME AL   Oh, Well, He Didn't Need It So Badly   By Ring Lardner

By Jack Keefe
(New White Sox Pitcher)

Well friends this is my 1st plung as a baseball writer but everybody has got to start some time and I figured I could not be no worse then the regular reporters. Well friends the sporting editor has ast me to give you a little dope on the natl. pastime of baseball so will say that it looks to me like as if the Yankees would have there hands full winning another pennant next yr. as all Gleason needed to make a bumb out of them was another star right hand pitcher witch I dont want to sound like I was boosting but I will stand this league on there head just like I done in the Central where I win the penant for Terre Haute single hand it you might say.

In my next article will write in regards to my different deliverys etc. and why the boys has such trouble hitting me so will close for this time.

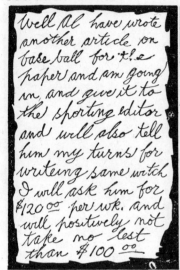

By Jack Keefe
(The New White Sox Pitcher)

Well friends the secret of my success as a pitcher is on acct. of the stuff I have got and further and more will say that when I am in there the batter never knows what is comeing next as I use my branes and genally always manage to outguest the boys and will say in this connection that I give my own sines while pitching and will insist on same even when pitching to the great little White Sox catcher Ray Schalk who I apreciate his ability but will not stand for no catcher telling me how to pitch.

Big league scouts who seen me work down in the Central League has told friends of mine that my fast ball reminds them of Walter Johnson at his best and my curve reminds them of 3 finger Brown wile have also got a delivery a good deal like Matty's fade away only more of a brake to it wile have also got a slow one witch I dont half to use often but will probly make a monkey out of Babe Ruth the king of swats.

So all and all I guess my readers will see that I am not brakeing into the big league empty hand it like so many young pitchers that is broughten up here and nobody knows why.

the Spring and worked cleverly

YOU KNOW ME AL   Valentino Has Nothing on Handsome Jack.   By Ring Lardner

By Jack Keefe
(New White Sox Pitcher)

Well friends the sporting editor has ast me would I write him a little article on the big city girls and what do I think of them. Well girls aint no different in the city than anywheres else as a few of them is pretty and the rest is homily. The most of them is wild over big stropping athaletes and bothers us to death with mash notes and etc. and down in the Central League why every town where we played in it kept us busy ducking them and I suppose it will be the same story up here.

Personly I will say without boosting that I have had my share of smiles from the fare sex and some of them mighty swell gals but I always figure that flirting dont get a man nothing till they make up there mind to get married and personly I aint met no dame yet who I would tie myself up to them and a specially now as this will be my 1st yr. in the big league and want to give Gleason the best I have got without no wife driving me ½ crazy with there quarls and etc.

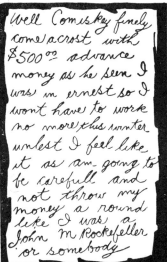

The Busher's Winter Loves

Well Al I guess I told you about going to a maskerade tomorrow night that dont start till midnight and everybody has got to ware a fancy costume and I couldent think what to ware till finely Julie says why dont you ware a White Sox uniform so I am going over to Comiskey's office this P.M. and borry 1 off them if they have got 1 big enough.

Her name is Edna Al and she is staring in a music show down to the Colonial and she went nuts over me and says I must come down and meet her at the stage door tomorrow night and take her somewheres to supper and maybe some time she will lern me to trip the light fanatic. How is that Al to have a actress crazy about you. Poor Julie acted pretty jellus and why not but could I help it.

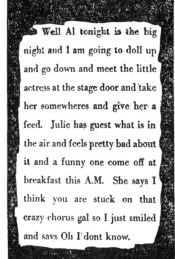

Well Al tonight is the big night and I am going to doll up and go down and meet the little actress at the stage door and take her somewheres and give her a feed. Julie has guest what is in the air and feels pretty bad about it and a funny one come off at breakfast this A.M. She says I think you are stuck on that crazy chorus gal so I just smiled and says Oh I dont know.

HERE'S MY BIG BOY! THIS IS MY FRIEND, MISS GABRIEL- DO YOU MIND IF SHE COMES ALONG?

THE MORE THE MERRIER!! ✦!

DO YOU WANT ME TO ORDER FOR US?   **GO AHEAD**

WELL, HOW ABOUT SOME OYSTERS, AND THEN SOME HORS D'OEUVRE, AND SQUAB, AND—

—HEARTS OF LETTUCE WITH RUSSIAN DRESSING, AND WE'LL ORDER DESSERT LATER

MAKE THAT FOR TWO-, I DONT NEVER EAT AT NIGHT!

Well Al the bill come to $11.80 and I had to tip the waiter to, witch made it $12.00 even. I would not of minded if she had not of broughten that other dame along as you cant have no fun when theys 2 of them. But she says if I come down again tomorrow night she would shake the other dame and give us a chance to talk to each other but you can bet it wont be at that jip joint where we was.

Friend Al, Well old pal I got another date with the little acterine tonight and this time they wont be no other gal along to spoil the party and will have a chance to maybe hold hands with Edna and I dont mind telling you Al that I am stuck on her and it looks like she had kind of took to me to or why would she want me around all the wile.

OH, HERE YOU ARE, BIG BOY! LET ME INTRODUCE FLOYD KNIGHT, ONE OF THE BOYS IN OUR SHOW!

12-30

WE THOUGHT WE'D GO TO SOME ITALIAN PLACE

(Copyright, 1922, by The Bell Syndicate, Inc.)

I FEEL LIKE SPAGHETTI AND CHEESE

YOU LOOK LIKE IT

WELL, GOOD NIGHT!

WHEN WILL I SEE YOU AGAIN, EDNA?

1-2

DO YOU LIKE OPERA?

I ONLY SEEN ONE— THAT'S "SALLY"

NO PARKING HERE

WELL, THERE'S A SPECIAL MATINEE OF IL TROVATORE THURSDAY

I'LL TRY AND GET TICKETS

(Copyright, 1922, by The Bell Syndicate, Inc.)

WHAT'S THE PRICES FOR TOMORROW'S MATINEE?

DOWNSTAIRS, $5.50— FIRST BALCONY $3.30— SECOND BALCONY $2.20·

TICK

Well Al I am going to take the little acterine to the grand opera Ill troubador tomorrow P.M. How is that for putting on the Dog and the 2 tickets cost me $4.40 as I got seats in the 2d. balcony because they say if you set down stares the piano plays so loud that you cant here the music.

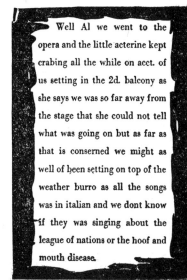

Well Al we went to the opera and the little acterine kept crabing all the while on acct. of us setting in the 2d. balcony as she says we was so far away from the stage that she could not tell what was going on but as far as that is conserned we might as well of been setting on top of the weather burro as all the songs was in italian and we dont know if they was singing about the league of nations or the hoof and mouth disease.

Well Al I am going to the show tomorrow night witch Edna Heath is the star of it and she is the little acterine who we are stuck on each other and I got a seat in the 1st. row and they soked me $4.40 witch is murder but a man cant stop to think about money when you are in love. I am also going to give her a suprise and buy her a bouquet and when she gets threw with her 1st. song I will toss it up on the stage and she will be crazer about me than ever.

How is that for a fine deal Al when I went and blowed myself to a bouquet for the little gal and have that big wash woman wipe her ft. on it and then they sweep it up like it was garbage or something. And then of course when I seen Edna after the show and told her about it she thought I was a fire and I had to buy her a swell feed to square myself. Dont never get stuck on a actress Al they are poison.

38

Well Al talk about a tough brake, I was comeing home on a st. car last night after seeing my little actress friend to her hotel and 1 of these here dips must of picked my pocket or something and took my whole role and left me flatterer than northern Indiana so I wundered if you could leave me have $75.00 or a $100.00 right away and will send it back in a mo. or 2 weeks at the outside. Please do this Al as you know I would give you my shirt only it would be to big for you.

Edna Heath the little actress gal who I told you about that I am stuck on, she took me to supper and paid the check herself witch was over $5.00 and she insisted on loning me a 5 spot and she says I was a good fellow only silly and why dident I get a job somewheres. How is that for a big heart Al and anybody that says chorus gals aint got no heart is a ½ wit but how she knowed I was clean is a misery to me.

What do you think Al, your old pal is going to be a actor and it aint no chorus man job neither but I am going to play the part of a policeman. The man they had got hurt and they want a big stropping man to play the part. It is in the same show with little Edna the chorus gal I been going with and she got me the job and I will have some lines to say so it looks like big money.

Well Al just a line as I have got to rush down to the theater as the stage mgr. is going to give me a rehearsal in the part witch my little actress friend Edna got for me in her show. She gets $30.00 per wk. and is just a chorus gal with nothing to say but I am going to play the part of a policeman and will half to lern some lines so it looks like I could comand about a $100.00 per wk. salery or $80.00 at the most so never mind about loning me that $75.00 smackers.

Well Al it is after supper and I am waiting for the time to go to the theater as I am going to play my part for the 1st. time tonight and we rehearsed this P. M. and the star comedian prased me and said I done great. But they aint much to the part only I say 1 line to him and he pretends like he hits me and I fall, only I got to lern to fall without getting hurt as suppose I was to hurt the old right arm. Where would I be at Al or the White Sox either?

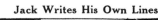

Well Al here is what come off. I was suppose to say he was under arrest but I was kind of nervous and I said it wrong and he got sore and realy hit me instead of pertending, so I lost my head and knocked him for a mile of side track. But you ought to heard the audience holler and laugh and when I come off the stage the chorus gals wanted to kiss me as nobody likes this ham. So I dont know if I am going to perform again Monday or not but I know he aint.

41

She Ought to Have Been Fired for That

BUT LISTEN, I'M ONE OF THE ACTORS, I PLAY A POLICEMAN!

STAGE DOOR

THEY'VE CUT OUT THE POLICEMAN- IT MADE TOO MANY STAR PARTS

STAGE DOOR

I'M FIRED, TOO!

WHAT FOR, EDNA?

DOOR

FOR TELLING THEM YOU WAS AN ACTOR

So they have give both of us the air Al and personly I am glad of it as far as I am conserned personly because stage-life may be O. K. for willy boys that powders there nose but it aint no place for a big stropping he man like I. But I feel sorry for the little gal and it was this back biting comedian Meyers that done it and he is suppose to make people laugh but if I ever catch a hold of him the laugh will be on the other ft.

Mr. Meyers "Goes Over Big" Again

Well Al I dident sleep a wink all night and lade awake worring about my little actress friend that got fired out of her show on acct. of trying to do me a flavor and I am going down to the hotel where she is stopping at and pull a few of my gags on her and try to cheer her up and make her forget. And afterwards I am going over to the theater and lay for this comedian Meyers and he wont feel so comical when I get threw with him.

YOU LOANED ME $5 WHEN I WAS FLAT SO I AM GOING TO RETURN THE FAVOR, EDNA

MAKE IT AS MUCH AS YOU CAN AND I WILL PAY YOU BACK TOMORROW

HERE IS ALL I GOT, $85

THAT'S A GOOD OLD PAL!

WELL, FOR ONCE, CORA, I WENT OVER BIG!

STAGE DOOR

THAT MAKES IT TWICE!

STAGE DOOR

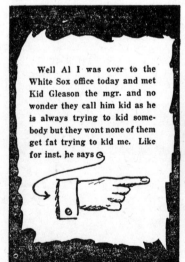

YOU KNOW ME AL

Schalk Looks at the Pitcher on the Slab

—By RING LARDNER

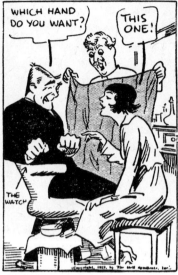

Kid Gleason the mgr. of the White Sox has went back east and wont be in Chi again till time to start for Texas. We had a long talk before he left and he says if I was you I would not wait for no training trip but would start in now and exercise every day because we have got a spring serious with the N. Y. giants the champions of the world and I am depending on you to make a sucker out of them. So I says I could beat them tomorrow but he says he was afrade it was to late to get up a game. He was kidding Al but any way I am going to start light exercise so as I will be in shape when we play the giants and they will be lucky to get a foul off of me.

I'M JACK KEEFE OF THE WHITE SOX

DID YOU WANT A GLOVE OR SOME SHOES OR SOMETHING?

1-24

NO, I WANT SOMETHING TO EXERCISE WITH - GLEASON WANTS ME TO GET MY ARM IN SHAPE SO AS I CAN TRIM THE GIANTS DOWN SOUTH!

DID YOU EVER WORK WITH DUMB-BELLS?

DID I ? SAY, THEY WAS AN INFIELDER ON OUR CLUB LAST YEAR THAT THOUGHT THE FIRST BOUNCE WAS STILL OUT!

Well Al I have boughten me a pare of dumbells and some indian clubs and I am going to exercise a hr. a day with them so as to get my mussles hard and I will have a start on the rest of the boys when we go south and if Gleason trys to wrestle with me again he will think he has bumped up vs. Stranger Lewis or somebody.

1-25

HOO 'RAY! JACK!

Jack Is a Shrinking Violet

I had my palm red by 1 of these here fortune tellers and of coarse the most of them is the bunk but they was nothing foney about this 1 as she says the gals was wild about me but I got to much sence to swell up. She also says I was going to get a hold of some money in a day or 2 from a unexpected sorce which I hope she is right about that to as I am flat and will half to buy some close before the ball club starts for Texas. 1 thing sure Al no matter where the money comes from it will be unexpected. Jokeing to 1 side Al I wonder if you could lone me a $100.00 dollars till our 1st. pay day and I would be ever so much oblige.
                    Jack Keefe

Jack Still Lives in Expectations

Well Al she was a swell looking dame and if they was real perls they must of been worth a hole lot of money but instead of giveing me a couple berrys she even acted like it hurt her mouth to say thanks. And the minute she said they was perls I thought about what that fortune teller told me that I was going to get some money from a unexpected sorce. But women dont never give you nothing Al and its a wonder they aint all umpires.

46

Your letter recd. Al and sorry to here you are hard up and cant lone me no money though it would only be till the 15 of April, I been kind of waiting in the hopes that what the fortune teller told me would come true namely that I would get some money from a unexpected sorce but it looks like she wasent no better guesser then some of them boys that called balls and strikes in our league last summer. I am going over to the ball pk. this P.M. and ask Comiskey to advance me another $100.00 dollars but from the way he acted last time I got as much chance as a left handed 3d. baseman.
Jack Keefe.

$"NO!"$

NO, COMISKEY ISN'T IN — BUT LISTEN, I OPENED A LETTER OF YOURS THIS MORNING BY MISTAKE AND IT'S FROM MRS. STANLEY POWELL

2-14

SHE'S THE SOCIETY LEADER OF CHICAGO AND SHE WANTS YOU TO CALL AT HER HOME

YOU DON'T KNOW HER, DO YOU?

NO, BUT THAT DON'T MAKE NO DIFFERENCE TO THEM DAMES

SHE PROBABLY GOT A LOOK AT ME SOMEWHERES AND IT WAS GOOD NIGHT!

Well Al I got a mash note yesterday from a dame name Mrs. Stanley Powell who they tell me she is the socitey leader of Chi and ast would I come and call on her. How is that for hitting the high spots and I dont know her but she must of seen me on the st. or somewheres and ast who I was. Well I will call on her if that will do her any good but wont give her no encouragements. Mean wile I aint seen nothing of all that money which the fortune teller said I was going to get and the next time anybody offers to tell my fortune I will offer them a punch in the jaw.
Jack Keefe.

I COME TO SEE MRS. POWELL

MRS. POWELL IS OUT

2-15

MY NAME IS JACK KEEFE — SHE AST ME TO CALL ON HER

OH YES! YOU ARE THE MAN WHO FOUND HER PEARL NECKLACE

MRS. POWELL SAID TO GIVE YOU THAT

??

$1,000

I bet you will be suprised when you here what come off. Do you remember me writing you the other day about a fortune teller saying I would get money from a unexpected sorce? And the next day I seen a swell dame drop her perl necklace in the park and I give it back to her and all she done was say thanks. But she took my name and the next day I got a note to call on Mrs. Stanley Powell the socitey leader of Chi and I thought it was just some dame that was stuck on me but it was her who I found the necklace. And what do you think she give me? Well Al you wont never guess so may as well tell you it was a $1000.00 dollar bill and I would go down and kiss that fortune teller only she is a 100 yrs. old and I showed Lefty Allen the bill and he says to stick it in a bank before I loose it so I am going down town and find a bank that looks like they was relible. Jack Keefe.

Well Al you know that $1000.00 bill which the woman give me for finding her perl necklace. Well I have stuck it in a bank and they give me a check book and any time I want a little money all as I do is write out a check and sine my name and the bank will half to come acrost with the amt. or I will make it hot for them. But beleive me I aint going to spend only what is nessary and 1st. thing is to buy some close to ware on the training trip which us pitchers is going a head of the rest of the club on the 26 of Feb. and I am going to buy 2 bran new suits to flash on them Texas dames and I dont care if they cost $35. a peace because when a man gets to be a big leaguer Al they ought to look the part. Jack Keefe.

Well Al just 1 wk. from to-day and we will be on the board of the old rattler bound for Sunny Texas. I am going down town this P. M. and buy me some new close as they say some of the other boys on the White Sox is reglar duds and I dont want to be showed up my 1st yr. in fast Co. You under-stand that is just a joke Al as a man with a physeek like mine looks good in anything you might say but just the same I am going to have a couple suits made to order by a taylor and they soke a man something feirce but what is $35.00 dollars per suit if it sends me along with them southren bells?

Jack Keefe.

HERE IS SOMETHING THAT MAKES UP CLASSY AND IT'S ONLY $50

THAT'S TOO MUCH DOUGH

2-19

WE GIVE YOU AN EXTRA PAIR OF TROUSERS

BUT WHERE I WANT TO WEAR THE SUIT IS IN TEXAS!

I'D ROAST TO DEATH DOWN THERE IN TWO PAIR OF PANTS

I got fited yesterday for 2 new suits to ware on the training trip and the 2 of them is going to cost me $80.00 but the taylor guaran-tees them to not shrink or turn color and he took all my meas-ures so as they will be sure and fit and it is to bad you aint got a taylor like he down home Al so you could have your close made to order and not look all the wile like you had stole a old suit off President Taft or somebody. Today I half to buy some new shirts and collars and etc. and I guess when them Texas bells sees me they will wonder when the White Sox signed Valentino.

Jack Keefe.

BUT IF YOU WEAR A 16 SHIRT, YOU DON'T WANT A 17 COLLAR!

2-20

I TRIED 16½ ONCE BUT THEY CUT THE OLD APPLE

HOW ABOUT NIGHT SHIRTS?

I GOT ONE!

I was talking to Julie the land-ladys daughter where I board and sprung it on her about us leaveing for Texas next Monday and she just as much as said she would go along if I and her was marred. Well Al she was talking to the wrong horse that time as I am not going to have no wife on my sholders wile I am trying to break in to big league baseball and besides I heard her tell her mother a few days ago that she was haveing a lot of trouble with her teeth. I always figured that a man would be a sucker to get marred at my age even if there gal was O. K. let alone when her teeth has got to be over halled.

Jack Keefe.

Well Al I read in the paper this A. M. that Bill Lane had reported to Comiskey and he was in the westren league last yr. and he is a right hand pitcher and the paper says that Mgr. Gleason fig-ured he had the best chance to make good of any of the young White Sox pitchers. Well let them rave Al but anyway I am going over to the ball pk. this P. M. and maybe this bird will be there and I will see what he looks like and of coarse you cant tell how he can pitch by his looks but I can tell if he has got brains and if he aint why he better go back to the westren league where they aint nessary.

Jack Keefe.

The Busher Starts the Season

Such Is Fame —By RING LARDNER

Only got time for a line Al as must get my bagage ready as we are leaving tonight for Marlin, Tex. Comiskey is sending the pitchers and catchers ahead of the rest of the club so as we can get in shape for the spring serious with the N. Y. giants and they are sending Ray Schalk the catcher in charge of us and he says to all be at the station a ½ hr. ahead of time but I aint going to be there till the last minute as they will be a big crowd of fans to see us off and I aint the kind that is looking for the line light. You know me Al.
JACK KEEFE.

2-26

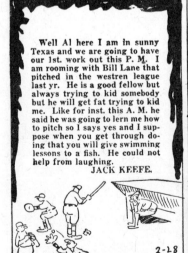

Might as Well Begin Practice —By RING LARDNER

Well Al here I am in sunny Texas and we are going to have our 1st. work out this P. M. I am rooming with Bill Lane that pitched in the westren league last yr. He is a good fellow but always trying to kid somebody but he will get fat trying to kid me. Like for inst. this A. M. he said he was going to lern me how to pitch so I says yes and I suppose when you get through doing that you will give swimming lessons to a fish. He could not help from laughing.
JACK KEEFE.

2-28

Well Al what do you think? One of the baseball writers from Chi that is here in Marlin with us wants I should write a 100 wds. a day in regards to what we are doing and etc. and he says his paper will pay me $20.00 per wk. for same. That is just like fining money as writeing comes as easy to me as pitching and I can tare off a 100 wds. like Jack Robinson. So after this Al you look in the paper evry day and you will see what Jack Keefe has got to say about the old White Sox. Today we are going to have a little batting practice and maybe I will show Schalk that I can do something besides pitch.

BY JACK KEEFE
Recruit White Sox Pitcher

Marlin, Tex., March 5—Well freinds the editor of this paper has ast me to wire a 100 wd. telegram evry night in regards to what the White Sox boys is doing on there training trip. As no doubt the fans knows by this time I am one of Comiskeys young pitchers boughten last yr. from Terre Haute where I practially win the penant single handed you might say but will try and not talk about myself but will give the other boys a square deal. So far only 1 or 2 of the young pitchers looks like they had a chance. So far Ray Schalk the catcher has been in charge of us but tomorrow Mgr. Gleason himself will be here and wile Schalk has did fairly good as a mgr. still one in all will be glad to see Mgr. Gleason who we call the kid on acct. of always trying to kid somebody. More tomorrow.

BY JACK KEEFE
Recruit White Sox Pitcher

Marlin, Tex., March 6.—Mgr. Kid Gleason has arrived on the seen and has took charge of the boys and soon we will know who is who and a man cant help from feeling sorry for some of the boys that is suppose to be pitchers but the scout that recommended them was either there brother in law or else X eyed. Personly the Kid seems to of took a fancy to yrs. truly and always hanging a round me and we have a great time kidding each other back and 4th. The White Sox mgr. is a great kidder but when the 2 of us gets together it is like greek meeting another greek.

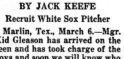

BY JACK KEEFE
Recruit White Sox Pitcher.

Marlin, Tex., March 7—Only 2 more days and the White Sox pitchers and catchers will brake camp here and move over to Seguin where we will join the rest of the squad and get ready for the big serious with the N. Y. giants. Needles to say Mgr. Gleason is anxious to beat the giants and I suppose the fans of Chi feels the same way and can assure them that when I face McGraw's men I will do my best which I often say that is the best any man can do though you take some of the other young pitchers on the squad and even when they are doing there best you would think the game of baseball was a big supprise to them.

BY JACK KEEFE
Recruit White Sox Pitcher

Marlin, Tex., March 8—The boys is getting packed up to leave here in rout for Seguin where we will join the rest of the boys. Tomorrow A.M. is our last day in Marlin and Mgr. Gleason says he won't ask none of we pitchers to do any more throwing for the fear we might strane our arm as he wants us to all be in shape to give the regulars plenty of batting practice next wk. How ever he has ast everybody to report at the ball pk. tomorrow and run around the pk. to strenthen there wind. Personly my wind is O.K. and am in shape right now to go the full rout but from what I seen of some of the other recrutes they better strenthen there wind as they will soon half to walk back to the different leagues they come from.

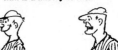

BY JACK KEEFE
Recruit White Sox Pitcher

Seguin, Tex., March 9—Well friends here we are at Seguin and the rest of the boys was here to meet us and I suppose the fans in old Chi will want to know if any of we young pitchers showed up good enough at Marlin so as to win a place on Mgr. Gleason's staff. Well some of the boys showed they had the stuff wile others won't never do and wile I won't mention no names, why it looks to me like they was 1 young pitcher who Gleason will soon ship him back to the westren league where he belongs and how any big league scout ever seen fit to reccomend a man like him is a misery to me.

BY JACK KEEFE
Recruit White Sox Pitcher

Seguin, Tex., March 11—The entire squad got together for the 1st time today and some of we young pitchers throwed to the batters to give them practice and I wished you could of seen some of the old timers pop there eyes out when I cut lose with my fast ball. I was a triffle wild but will get over that with more work. Tomorrow we are going to play a real game with the regulars vs. the yanigans and Mgr. Gleason has ast me to pitch the 1st 3 innings vs. the regulars and if I am right they wont get a foul.

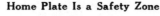

BY JACK KEEFE
Recruit White Sox Pitcher

Seguin, Tex., March 12—Well the yanigans drawed 1st blood as we beat the regulars in the 1st game by a score of 3 to 0 and I pitched the 1st 3 innings and they would not of had a hit only for Flynn our left fielder pulling a boner. In the 2d innings Schalk hits a fly ball to left field which a girl could of catched but Flynn lets it fall safe and I guess he must of came from a league where the 1st bounce is still out. Any way we win the ball game and after the game I says to Gleason you ought to call us the regulars and call them the yanigans. I guess your right he says smiling.

BY JACK KEEFE
Recruit White Sox Pitcher

Seguin, Tex., March 15—Well we go to San Antone Saturday to start the big serious with the N. Y. giants and today I had a kidding match about the serious with Mgr. Gleason. He says he might start me in the 1st game and I says leave me pitch the entire game and he says no because he was afrade they would quit. So I says who the giants? No he says my outfielders.

Tomorrow we are going to have another game between the regulars vs. the yanigans witch will be our last practice before the big serious.

BY JACK KEEFE
Recruit White Sox Pitcher

Seguin, Tex., March 20—Well friends I suppose you read in the papers where I give 8 bases in that game with the N. Y. giants but I hope you Chicago fans wont be worred on that acct. as I was not trying very hard as these games does not count and besides they was a Natl. league umpire behind the plate and would not call a strike unlest the batter swang at it twicet but it will be a different story next time and today it is raining and some of the boys has ast me to play cards.

3-20

I WISHT WE HAD SOME BEER

SHUT UP

THEY'S ONLY FOUR OF US. WE BETTER PLAY DEUCES WILD

WHAT DO YOU MEAN, WILD?

SAY, IF THEY'S ONE GUY IN THE WORLD THAT OUGHT TO KNOW WHAT WILD MEANS, YOU'RE IT!

BY JACK KEEFE
Recruit White Sox Pitcher.

Seguin, Tex., March 21—Well I give the N. Y. giants a touch of high life today and held them to 1 run in 5 innings and they would not of got that 1 only Mostil misjudged a fly ball and give this here Frisch a 2 base hit and then I let him steal 3d. and home as these games dont count for nothing any way and what is 1 run any way? I figured 1 run wouldent never win that game and sure enough we got a couple runs in the 8th. inningg and beat them 2 to 1.

3-22

THROW HOME

THROW THAT APPLE

THROW IT!

SAFE!!

BALL

FRISCH

WHAT DO YOU MEAN, TAKING A WIND-UP LIKE THAT WITH A MAN ON THIRD BASE?

I THOUGHT HE WAS STILL ON SECOND

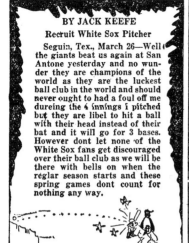

BY JACK KEEFE
Recruit White Sox Pitcher

Seguin, Tex., March 26—Well the giants beat us again at San Antone yesterday and no wunder they are champions of the world as they are the luckest ball club in the world and should never ought to had a foul off me dureing the 4 innings I pitched but they are libel to hit a ball with their head instead of their bat and it will go for 3 bases. However dont let none of the White Sox fans get discouraged over their ball club as we will be there with bells on when the reglar season starts and these spring games dont count for nothing any way.

3-26

Friend Al:—

Well Al since the last time I write you they have give me a new room mate in the stead of Bill Lane who I am glad to get rid of him as he is jellus as he knows I have got him beat to death and the only chance he has got to stay with the White Sox is suppose I should die. My new roomy is a young outfielder name Whelan from the coast league and a nice boy only he cant go back after a fly ball or go in after them and if he comes up to bat second in a inning it is 2 out. But he aint no smart Alex like Bill Lane.

61

Friend Al:

Well Al Gleason says I have got to pitch vs. the N. Y. giants again tomorrow and the only guy they have got who can hit what I have got is this guy Frisch and I can fool him to death as one of their own men has told me his weakness. This man hates him and he says if I ever want to make a sucker out of Frisch to pitch him a low curve ball inside. So that is what this baby is going to get the next time I pitch vs. him.

3-30

'YOU KNOW ME AL'   By Ring Lardner

BY JACK KEEFE
Recruit White Sox Pitcher

Dallas, Tex., March 31—Well friends I never would of loose this game to the giants only for Schalk and when Young come up in the 8 innings I wanted to give him a curve ball but Schalk insisted on a fast one and Young hits it out of the ball pk. and if that is getting any help out of your catcher I am nuty and the next time you can bet that I wont pay no tension to a catcher just because they have got a reputation.

Friend Al— Well Al this is the big day when I start my big league carrier as Gleason says I have got to start to day's game vs. the Indians. Well Al I will give them the best I have got and often say that is the best anybody can do and I ast him why they call them the Indians and he says because they are wild but they have got nothing on you. Well Al I will show them if they are wild or not and you can fine out how I come out in tomorrow's papers.

Resky. Jack Keefe

4-20

NOW FORGET WHO THESE GUYS ARE AND PITCH JUST LIKE YOU WAS PITCHING AGAINST SOME BUSH LEAGUE CLUB

THREE BAGGER

WHEN I TOLD YOU TO WALK SPEAKER, WHY DIDN'T YOU?

YOU TOLD ME TO **FORGET** WHO THESE GUYS WAS, AND I DID!

CLEVELAND	3	6	4
CHICAGO	0	0	0

4-21

WELL, I DON'T BELIEVE NOBODY WIN THE PRIZE

WHAT PRIZE?

THE PRIZE FOR GUESSING HOW YOUR FIRST GAME WOULD COME OUT

ROCKEFELLER DIDN'T MAKE NO GUESS

AND HE'S THE ONLY ONE THAT COULD THINK IN THOSE KIND OF FIGURES

63

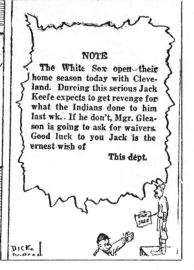

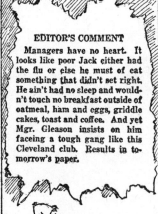

64

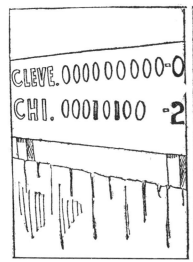

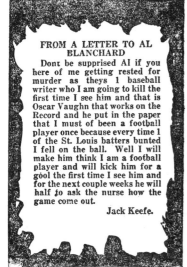

EDITORIAL

It does seem kind of sad that some nice gal don't take a fancy to a handsome boy like Jack Keefe who has all ready pitched 3 games in the big league and only lose 2 and when he takes a gal out to dinner he always says put it all on one check. This is a great chance for the right kind of a gal and it looks to me like you dames was making a big mistake overlooking this well favored goofer.

The Busher's Courtship

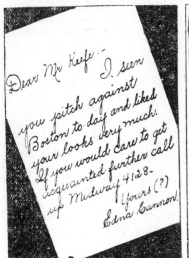

'YOU KNOW ME AL' — By Ring Lardner

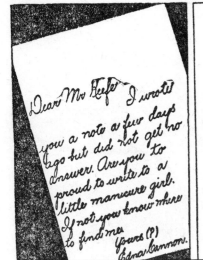

68

Correspondence

Dear Miss Cannon:

Am sorry to say I will not have no time to look you up before leaving for Detroit but maybe will look you up when we get back home and mean wile will be glad to here from you and would be glad if you would send me your photo, also tell me something about yourself and how you come to get interested in me and etc. Will expect letter and photo from you wile we are in Detroit and may give you a ring when we get home witch will be next Mon.

Respy,
Jack Keefe.

Correspondence

Dear Mr. Keefe:

I certainly was glad to hear from you at last. Am enclosing the only picture I have got of myself and it is just a little snap shot taken last summer at South Haven where a girl friend and myself spent our vacation last summer. My friends say it does not do me justice but "needles" to say they may be just "jolly-ing" me. But you can judge for yourself when you see me "face to face" which I hope will be as soon as you get back to "old Chi." Mean time please write and tell me that you don't think me "ug-ly" even if the picture is crazy looking. Would have a real photo of myself only I *hate* having my picture taken as it makes a person seem like they were concieted. Yours (?)
Edna Cannon.

YOU KNOW ME AL

Aha! Jack Is Falling for the Vamp

—By RING W. LARDNER

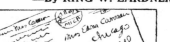

Correspondence

Dear Miss Cannon,

Your letter encloseing photo recd. Maybe the photo dont flatten you but it sure looks good to me only cant tell from it if you are blond or dark and wished you would write and tell me something about yourself. De-troit is a great town and got a great ball club but I made them look like a monkey today and they shouldent of never had that 1 run.

Jack Keefe.

Correspondence

Dear Mr. Keefe:

You certainly are an old "curiosity shop" wanting to know if I am a blonde or brunette. Well Mr. Curious I am a brunette with wavy hair almost black and dark brown eyes and some of my friends have told me how much I look like Pola Negri though personally I cannot see much resemblance though I certainly wish I did look like her as I think she is beautiful. But maybe you prefer blondes. Do you, Mr. Keefe? If you do I am sorry but afraid it is "too late" to change. But if you can "stand for" a little brunette who is a great admire of yours, why you know where to find me and will expect to hear from you as soon as you get back to "old Chi."

Yours (?)
Edna Cannon.

YOU KNOW ME AL   *Too Much Mustard!*   **—By RING W. LARDNER**

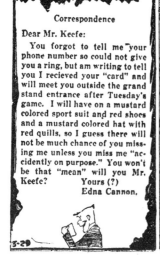

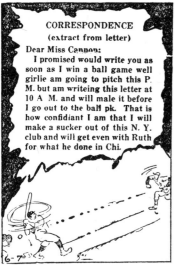

You Know Me Al

Seven Days of Rest for Them

By Ring Lardner

YOU KNOW ME AL ❧ ❧ ❧ ❧ By Ring Lardner

CORRESPONDENCE

Dear Miss Cannon:

This is our last day in Boston and leave right after the game for Washington. I said I would write you a letter as soon as I win a game, well am going to pitch against Boston today and if I cant beat them will quit pitching but any way will male this letter as I know how you must feel not herring from me except post cards. Well girlie will expect to here from you in Washington and mean wile dont take no bad money.

Jack Keefe

CORRESPONDENCE

Dear Mr. Keefe:

Just a line to tell you about a dream I had last night. I dreamt it was a world series game in Chi and the crowd was carrying you off the field on their shoulders. Do you beleive in dreams and would not it be grand was my dream to come true? You owe me a letter so will not write any more now, but felt like I must tell you about the dream.

Yours (?)

Edna Cannon.

77

Correspondence.

Dear Mr. Keefe:

I feel so lonesome and blue and thought maybe it would cheer me up to write you a letter. You have no idea how lonesome a girl gets living all alone in a city like Chi and I feel sometimes like I would marry any man that asked me just so I would not have to live alone. Of course I don't mean that as I would never marry a man unless I cared for them, but it would be so nice to think there was someone somewheres that belonged to you even if they were on the road half the time. Will close now or you will think me a f----l.

Edna Cannon.

Correspondence

Dear Mr. Keefe:

Recieved your note from Cleveland and certainly envy you seeing all those points of interest like Mr. Rockefeller's home etc. but if I was a man like you I would not wish for Mr. Rockefeller's money. After all Mr. Keefe money is not everything and I would never marry a man personally for their money, but no matter how poor he was I would marry them if I loved them, that is of course if he wanted me. But you will think me an "it" if I "rave on" this way so will say "farewell" for this time.

Yours (?)

Edna Cannon

The Way to a Man's Heart

Jack Does a Hasty Scrawl

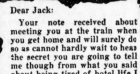

Dear Jack:

Your note received about meeting you at the train when you get home and will surely do so as cannot hardly wait to hear the secret you are going to tell me though from what you said about being tired of hotel life I think maybe I can guess what it is. I know how it feels to be lonesome and not have a home and I do hope—but there I would better not go on as I might be wrong about your secret and you would think me a little f--l.

Yours (?)

Edna

SAY, LEFTY, WHAT DOES IT COST TO GET MARRIED?

OH, ABOUT TWO DOLLARS. BUT IT AIN'T THE ORIGINAL COST—IT'S THE UP KEEP

I GIVE MY MISSUS $250 A MONTH AND SHE PAYS ALL THE BILLS

AND WHAT DOES THAT LEAVE YOU AT THE END OF THE MONTH?

IT LEAVES ME DISCOURAGED

YOU SAID IF I MET YOU AT THE TRAIN, YOU'D HAVE A SECRET TO TELL ME

WELL IT AIN'T MUCH, ONLY I WAS WONDERIN' IF I AND YOU COULDN'T GET MARRIED

I'VE GOT TO KNOW ONE THING FIRST—DO YOU—DO YOU LIKE ME?

WELL, I DON'T GO AROUND PROPOSIN' TO GIRLS THAT MAKE ME SICK

Friend Al:

Well Al it is all fixed up and I and Edna is going to get marred in a secret next Wed. and I only wished you could be here to stand up with me but wont ask you as I know you would half to buy a decent looking suite of close. We are going to get marred in front of a juge and it will half to be in the A.M. as I may half to pitch vs. Washington in the P.M. and will make a sucker out of them Al as they are beat the minute they see me start to begin to warn up.

Jack Keefe

The Busher Takes a Wife

Friend Al:

This is the last time I will write to you as a single man as tomorrow I will be a marred man as the big event is going to take place at 10 A.M. tomorrow A.M. when Juge Burke is going to tie the not and have ast Eddie Whelan one of the ball players to stand up with me and he has promised to not tell Gleason nothing about it. I thought it would be kind of fun to get marred in my uniform but Edna made a squawk and said I would half to wear a business suite or she would not marry me. I suppose she wants to be sure I mean business.

Jack Keefe.

AND NOW I CLAIM THE RIGHT TO KISS THE BRIDE

AS FOR YOU, I'LL SAY YOU'RE LUCKY!

LUCKY! DID YOU READ ABOUT THAT GAME IN PHILLY, WHERE I HAD 'EM LICKED 2 AND 0 AND MOSTIL LOSE THAT BALL IN THE SUN?

DICK DORGAN.

WELL, DON'T WE GET NO WEDDING BREAKFAST?

BREAKFAST! IT'S PRETTY NEAR NOON!

THAT DON'T MAKE NO DIFFERENCE. WHEN A PERSON GETS MARRIED, THEY ARE SUPPOSED TO BUY A MEAL FOR THE WEDDING PARTY. AND THEY ALWAYS CALL IT BREAKFAST

BRING US COFFEE AND ROLLS FOR THREE

DICK DORGAN

Friend Al:

Well Al I am a marred man and everything went off great till after the ceremoney when this here Whelan who I ast him to stand up with me insist it on me buying him his breakfast though it was pretty closet to 1 P. M. and cost me $.75 includeing tip and by the time we was threw eating it was time to go over to the ball pk. and I did not have no chance to even kiss my own bribe. How is that for a fine wedding Al and if I ever get marred again I will chose a man to stand up with me that can get up early enough to have their breakfast 1st. and not try and stand up on a empty stomach.

Jack Keefe

Friend Al:

Well Al I and the little bribe are liveing in this hotel till I can fine a apt. somewheres and they are soking us $21.00 per wk. meals extra so all and all it will cost me a round $30.00 a wk. to live as Edna eats like a horse though she dont take no more exercise then a gate man on the Monon. Besides 3 squares a day she cant set threw a P.M. at the ball pk. without she has a couple hot dogs and a bag of pop corn and I suppose it will be worse on days when we play a double header. Most women is afrade they will get fat but she acts like she is afrade she wont. How she ever got along when she had to buy her own meals is a misery to me.

Jack Keefe.

Friend Al:

Well Al wifes is certainly a funny proposition and now Edna insists on me taking her along on the next eastern trip and if she cant go she will kill herself and etc. and if I ask Gleason if I can take her along he will kill me so I dont know witch one of us is going to die first and if I did take her along it would mean the pore house as she has got the nag of picking out places to eat where ham and eggs is $2.50 and ketchup a $.25 extra. And just think of them places in N.Y. city where they sock you $2.00 a peace for a cover charge even when its so hot that they dont nobody want covers.

Jack Keefe.

8-22

BUT SHE SAYS SHE WILL DIE IF SHE DON'T SEE ME FOR THREE WEEKS

LISTEN: YOU TELL HER THIS. THE SEASON'S GOING TO END THE FIRST WEEK IN OCTOBER AND THEN I WON'T SEE YOU AGAIN TILL MARCH

AND THAT THOUGHT IS ALL THAT KEEPS ME ALIVE ♥ ♥ ♥

OH, MR. GLEASON, WON'T YOU LET JACK TAKE ME ALONG ON THE EASTERN TRIP?

8-24

WELL, I'VE ALREADY SAID NO, BUT I WANT TO BE FAIR----

IF HE WINS HIS NEXT TWO GAMES HERE, HE CAN TAKE YOU ALONG

Friend Al:

Well Al after me telling Edna that Gleason did not want me to take her on the eastern trip what does she do but ast him herself and he says she could go along provide ft I win the next two games here at home. Well Al you know I would not throw no ball game for love and money but the two clubs which I will probly pitch vs. is Boston and Cleveland who I cant hardly help from beating them as they are scarred to death as soon as I begin to warm up and it will be just my luck to have the empires open their eyes and give me a square deal for once and I will win both games and Edna will go along on the trip and cost a bbl of money and if Id of knew what wifes was going to be, I would not of married none of them.

Jack Keefe.

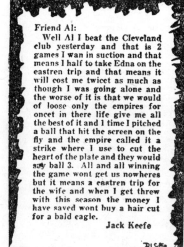

Friend Al:

Well Al I loose a tough luck game to the Detroit club yester-day or rather the empires loose-it for me as I never seen such empiring in my life and I dont see how some of these empires finds the ball pk as they are most of them stone blind. I felt like takeing a poke at one of them as he made a couple wise cracks tords me but I finely decide to not hit him but just talk back at him and you can guest who got the worst of the argument.

Jack Keefe.

"YOU KNOW ME AL."   It Is a Continuous Performance.   (Copyright, 1923.)   By Ring Lardner.

Friend Al:

Well Al we had a day off here today with no game schedule and its the 1st time Edna was ever in N.Y. city and she wanted I should hire a taxi and take her site seen but I says it would cost to much and we better walk so I guest we must of walked the whole lenth of 5th ave. and back and she says walking made her hungry and about every ½ hr. we would half to stop in some-wheres and get another meal and she did not pick out no cafe-terias niether and the next time she wants to go site seen I will hire the most expensive taxi in N.Y. and save money to say nothing about my poor dogs.

Jack Keefe.

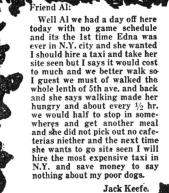

Friend Al:

Well Al what do you think of a woman who she wants you to sine up a least for a apt. for $2100.00 dollars per annum and my salery with the ball club is $2500.00 dollars per annum which would leaf $400.00 dollars for food and close and electric light and gas bill and etc. and if I ever wanted a hair cut I would half to give the barber a promisery note do in 5 or 6 yrs. Wifes is a great proposition Al and one of the ball players was telling me that they was a old saying that 2 could live as cheap as one but I guess who ever said it was thinking of gold fish or some other kind of a couple that dont half to pay no rent.

Jack Keefe.

Friend Al:

This is our last day at home and tonight we go to Cleveland to wine up the season and I ast Gleason to leave me stay home off the trip so as I could fine a place to live but he says you ether go to Cleveland with us and win a game there or else you wont need no place to live, not in this league any way. Well Al I aint scarred of Cleveland and will beat them sure but what I am scarred of is that wile I am gone Edna will sine up for some apt. that has got enough rooms to sleep the whole American legend. She has made up her mind that we must have a big place and when a woman makes up there mind they are worst then a umpire because you can at lease reason with a umpire without him bursting into tears.

Jack Keefe..

94

Friend Al:

Well Al I win my game from Cleveland today so for the whole season I have win 10 games and loose 8 and if the rest of our pitchers had did that good we would not of came so close to beating Boston out of last place. Gleason is leaveing me go home tonight so as I can look up a place to live though I told Edna to look a round wile I was gone and may-be she has got a place picked out so as we can move right in, which I will be tickled to death as I have been liveing in this hotel so long that pretty soon the guests will be asking me to fetch them some ice water.

Jack Keefe.

OH, I'VE RENTED THE DARLINGEST APARTMENT, JUST THIS SIDE OF EVANSTON!

WHY, THAT'S FIFTEEN MILES FROM THE BALL PARK!!

BUT IT'S GOT SIX ROOMS AND I'M GOING TO LET YOU HAVE ONE ALL TO YOURSELF!!

I WON'T NEED NO ROOM! I'LL SPEND MY NIGHTS IN SLEEPERS GOIN' TO AND FROM WORK!

Friend Al:

Well Al what do you think Edna pulled wile I was in Cleve-land, she went and least a 6 rm. apt. for 1 yr. and paid 1 mo. rent $125.00 in advance and the place is way up on the north side pretty near a sleeper jump from our ball pk. but the real estate man told her the view alone was worth the money as we are only a ½ a block from Lake Michigan and we can set right in our win-dow and look at the lake. Well Al from now on till the next baseball season I wont be mak-ing nothing per mo. let alone a $125.00 so when the real estate man comes around for the rent I will say I am sorry I cant pay you no cash but if you want to take it out in entertainment why you can set in our window all mo. and look at the lake.

Jack Keefe

THERE'S A GREAT, BIG CLOTHES CLOSET JUST FOR YOU AND I'M GOING TO BUY A LOT OF MOTH BALLS

YOU DON'T NEED TO BUY NO MOTH BALLS FOR MY CLOTHES CLOSET

MOTHS WON'T STAY WHERE THEY'S A FAMINE

Friend Al:

Well Al we got a night letter telegram this A. M. from Edna's sister Lottie saying she would arrive today to pay us a visit and Edna was so tickled she screened loud enough to wake up all the neighbors but personly I managed to hold myself in. The best of it is that Edna is going to be busy ranging the furniture in our new apt. and I will half to go down to the station and meet the sister and law and I suppose she will want to kiss me right in front of everybody but I wont mine nothing she does provide it she remembers she is just here for a visit and not no 99 yr. lease.

Jack Keefe

DEARIE, DON'T YOU THINK YOU OUGHT TO GET A JOB? IT SEEMS LIKE SOMEBODY IN THE FAMILY OUGHT TO BE EARNING SOMETHING!

WELL, THEY TELL ME IT'S EASIER FOR A WOMAN TO GET A JOB THAN A MAN

BUT IF SOME OF MY FRIENDS CAME TO SEE ME AND YOU TOLD THEM I WAS WORKING, WHAT WOULD THEY THINK?

THEY'D THINK I WAS A LIAR ?!

DICK DORGAN 10-26
(Copyright, 1923, by The Bell Syndicate, Inc.)

Friend Al:

Well Al what do you think of a man earning a big league salery of $2500.00 per yr. and now I have to go and look for a job or else we will wake up some A. M. and find out that we have moved to the poor house and I can remember when my old man sported 3 of us on $30.00 per mo. and still had enough left yet to get boiled every Saturday. But that was before wifes acted like the kitchen was haunted and before sister in laws thought that an invitation to visit was an annual pass. Well I guest I wont have no trouble getting a good position when I tell people whom I am but it seems a crime that a man like I should half to work dureing the off season when I ought to be giveing my brain a complete rest.
          Jack Keefe

WELL, HERE'S GOOD NEWS! JOE WHELAN'S COMIN' TO TOWN. HE WAS A EXTRA INFIELDER WE HAD WITH US LAST SUMMER. I AND HIM ROOMED TOGETHER.

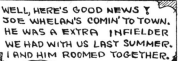

HE SAYS HE'S THINKING ABOUT GETTIN' MARRIED, BUT THEY AIN'T NO GAL IN HIS HOME TOWN THAT HE'D FALL FOR. SO HE'S COMIN' TO CHI TO LOOK FOR ONE.

WHAT IS HE LIKE?

DON'T GET EXCITED! HE'S THE HOMELIEST MAN IN THE WORLD. AND THE DUMBEST, AND HE MAKES ABOUT TWELVE HUNDRED A YEAR

(Copyright, 1923, by The Bell Syndicate, Inc.)

OH, BUT I DIDN'T TELL YOU ALL OF IT! HE'S IN ON A OIL LEASE AND HE'S ALREADY TURNED DOWN $30,000 FOR HIS SHARE!

WELL, HE REALLY ISN'T HOMELY; HE'S KIND OF CUTE LOOKING. AND HE SAYS THE MOST AMUSING THINGS!

DICK DORGAN 11-26

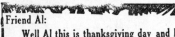

Friend Al:

Well Al this is thanksgiving day and I wished you and Bertha was here to have dinner with us as Edna has boughten a big turkey and all we got to eat it is her and myself and the sister in law and Joe Whelan who I guest I told you he had made a clean up in oil and this is the first time I will of saw him since the baseball season when he was getting $1200.00 a yr. and now he is worth over $30000.00 but thats the way it goes. All he done was set on the bench and keep it warm wile I got out and win a lot of ball games and here he is worth $30000.00 and I aint worth nothing. Thats the way it goes but I wished you and Bertha was here to help us eat up all this Turkey.

Jack Keefe

Fr:end Al:

Well Al we put it over. I just had a telegram from Joe Whelan down in Oklahoma saying that the oil least I invest it in has made good and a man has offered $17000.00 for my share. How is that for cleaning up Al and it just shows what a man can do with a little money if they are careful and dont go into things with there eyes shut. Whelan left Chicago about a wk. ago without saying nothing and Edna thought he had ran out with my $500.00 but I knowed he was not that kind and now the laugh is on her. He is comeing back to Chi in a couple days and we will split the dough and have a celebration but you can bet I am not going to throw my money away but will invest it in some good 2 or 3 per cent bond so as I will be on Easy st. the rest of my life even if my old arm goes back on me. Oh you little oil well.

Jack Keefe

Friend Al:

Well Al I just got a night letter telegram from Joe Whelan which he will be here today and is comeing out to the house and bring me a check for $17000.00 for my share of our little oil deel. Edna dont beleive it yet but I guest she will when she looks at the check which is all she is going to do is just look at it because if I was to indorst it over to her she would run down town and buy the post office bldg. But it looks like I would half to throw a big party tonight to kind of celebrate and show old Joe that I presiate what he has did for me. Wished you could be in on it Al but you might not feel comftable as we will probly hit some pretty swell joints.

Jack Keefe.

Friend Al:

Well Al we had some party last night and it cost me over $60.00 as Edna insist on we going to one of these here joints where you half to slip the head waiter a couple of $1.00 or you will set on the kitchen stove. And this here Joe Whelan did not make no offer to take none of the checks and I finely says to him I always did know that your arm was so weak that you half to throw twice to get the ball crost the diamond but I never knowed it was paralyzed so as you cant get it in your pocket. So Edna told him to not pay no tension to me, so I says you dont half to warn him to not pay no tension, he aint going to pay that or nothing else. On the way home she told me I ought to not of picked on him as he was tight, so I says that is why I was picking on him and she could not help from laughing.

Jack Keefe

Friend Al:

Well Al just a line to wisht you and Bertha a happy new yrs. and hope you have good luck all threw 1924. Dont that seem funny Al to say 1924 and I bet when I am dateing my checks and etc. I will put it 1923 on acct. of being use to it but after a wile I suppose a man will get use to putting it 1924. Any way Al here is best wishs for the new yr. and good luck and I know you are wishing me luck too though if my arm feels as good next spring as it does right now I wont need no luck.

Jack Keefe

JOE WHELAN CALLED UP AND WANTS US TO GO TO THE BELDEN WITH HIM TONIGHT AND WATCH THE NEW YEAR IN

HE SAYS IT'S HIS PARTY AND TO TELL YOU TO SAVE UP YOUR THIRST

OH, I WONDER IF WE'LL HAVE WINE!

WELL SIS, IF HE DOES BUY WINE, DON'T YOU DRINK TOO MUCH OF IT! YOU ALWAYS LOOK SO FUNNY!

DON'T WORRY! ALL THE WINE WHELAN'LL BUY WOULDN'T MAKE A GNAT CHANGE THEIR EXPRESSION!!

DICK DORGAN 12-31

COPYRIGHT 1923, BY THE BELL SYNDICATE, INC.

Friend Al:

Well Al what do you think Edna has did now, she has went and blowed $250.00 on one of these here radios that you are suppose to here music and speeches and etc. from N. Y. and San Francisco and all over and so far we had it 2 days and aint herd nothing only what sounds like a couple of cats nagging there husband. Edna says it will be O.K. when we get tuned in right but imagine anybody thinking that you could here somebody talking miles away when we aint got no wires or nothing except a couple boxs and some close line strung on a real and I suppose the next thing they will be selling us will be a plaster cast that you can put over your nose and smell the beer they are drinking in Germany.

Jack Keefe

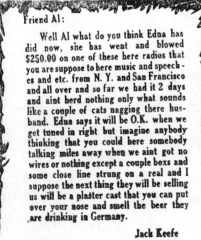

WELL, IS SHE TUNED IN YET?

THERE'S NOTHING ON NOW. BUT YOU OUGHT TO HAVE BEEN HERE A WHILE AGO. WE HAD WTAS! THAT'S ELGIN!

AND SIS AND I TOOK TURNS LISTENING TO THE SPEECHES AT A KIWANIS CLUB DINNER

I WISHED YOU HADN'T TOLD ME! I WON'T NEVER DAST LEAVE HOME AGAIN!!

DICK DORGAN 1-30-24

(Copyright, 1924, by The Bell Syndicate, Inc.)

Friend Al:

Well Al we are in swell socitey now and tonight we are going to the grand opera so it looks like we was in swell society. But we would not be going Al only a friend of Lotties give her 3 passes for the best seats so we will half to doll up and broad A each other and pertend like we was disgusting the different actors and dont you think Eva Tanguay is off the key tonight and etc. Well Al if I live threw it I will write and tell you what it was like and whether you missed anything but if you tell any of the boys aroud home about me going be sure they understand that I aint paying for it as I dont want them to think theys anything wrong.

Jack Keefe

HOW LONG HAS THIS OPERA BEEN RUNNIN' THAT WE'RE GOIN' TO SEE

WHY IT HASN'T BEEN 'RUNNING' AT ALL. THEY HAVE A DIFFERENT OPERA EVERY NIGHT.

GOSH! YOU'D THINK BY THIS TIME THEY'D OF GOT A HOLD OF A HIT

DICK DORGAN
(Copyright, 1924, by The Bell Syndicate, Inc.) 2-5-24

HOW MANY MORE ACTS IS THEY?

TWO I THINK. BUT PLEASE DON'T TALK SO LOUD!

WHAT DID YOU MAKE ME WEAR A DRESS SUIT FOR? WHAT A MAN OUGHT TO WEAR TO GRAND OPERA IS A NIGHTGOWN, SO HE COULD SLEEP MORE COMFORTABLER

WELL, YOU CAN BET THIS IS THE LAST TIME I'LL EVER ATTEND THE GRAND OPERA WITH YOO!

!

I KNOWED THAT BEFORE YOU DID

(Copyright, 1924, by The Bell Syndicate, Inc.)

Friend Al:

Well Al we went to the opera last night like I told you we was going to and it was a opera named Butterfly which I guest some other kind of a insect must of wrote it and any way the plot is about a lt. in the U. S. navy that goes to Japan and gets stuck on a Jap gal and they talk to each other in nothing but Italian. If that dont win a scholarship to the insane asylum why I am a left handed third baseman. Dont never leave nobody coax you in to going to the opera Al but theys one good thing about it, it makes a man feel lest jellus of rich people if that is the way they have got to put in there winters.

Jack Keefe

DICK DORGAN.- 2-7-24

105

Friend Al:

Well Al we are having a party tonight and when I was a kid why I use to think partys was the greatest thing in the world but now days I would just as leaf go to a funeral and I guest maybe I am getting old or something but it seems to me like people dont have good times no more like they use to and a specially when they invite people lik Edna has invited tonight. Joe Whelan is coming and he is O.K. but besides him theys a marred couple named Mr. and Mrs. Foley who Edna picked her up at a card party somewheres and Foley is the kind that knows everything and whatever you tell him he has got something to top it and if you mention the phonograph, why he was the one that give Robert E. Edison the idear. Well Al I and him gets along like Europe and it is all as I can do to keep from busting him so you can see what kind of a pleasant evening we are going to have.

Jack Keefe

106

Friend Al:

Well Al only a couple weeks and we will be off on the training trip to Florida and no more cold weather for your old pal for 9 months at lease and longer than that because I wont live around here another winter till somebody builds a apt. building that the architect wasent a eskimo. Wile we are south I am going to ask Mgr. Chance for 2 or 3 days off and hire a car and visit some of the other Florida towns and see if I cant invest in a little cottage for next winter somewheres. Joe Whelan says he heard that Palm Beach was the best place to pick up bargains and that the Flagler cottage down there was for sale and a big bargain so I will see what it looks like and is it big enough though I guest if it aint big enough for 2 people they would not call it a cottage but a corset or something.

Jack Keefe

Friend Al:

Well Al I thought it was cold enough in our apt. when it was just the weather that was cold but the weather wasent nothing compared to Edna since I told her she could not go along on the training trip. She wont speak to me or answer me when I talk to her and when ever I wan to say something I half to talk threw her sister just like as if I and my wife was foreigners to each other and spoke a different language and Lottie acts like a go between and translates what we say back and 4th. Sometimes it sounds funny Al and I pretty near half to laugh but if I laughed it would start a blizzard of books and chairs and etc. as she aint in no mode to see a joke.

Jack Keefe

The Busher's Second Year

Friend Al·

Well Al here I am in sonny Florida and weather just like June to hot for heavy underclose so am waiting for my trunk so can get in to summer under close. Also would like to try out some of them doggy sport close I bought in Chi as I notice theys some swell dames in this little old berg though of course they aint going to worry me now as I am a old marred man but can help it if they stair at me hey Al?

Theys a little gal here in the writing rm. right now that acts like she would talk to me if I give her the eye but am not the kind that forgets there family as soon as I get away from home and besides which dont want to raze no false hopes.

Jack Keefe

PARDON ME, BUT AREN'T YOU MR. KEEFE OF THE CHICAGO WHITE SOX?

YES, MA'AM

WELL, I'M MISS GALVIN OF THE WINTER HAVEN REALTY COMPANY. I THOUGHT I MIGHT INTEREST YOU IN BUYING A PERMANENT HOME HERE

MR. WHELAN TOLD ME HE OVERHEARD MR. EVERS SAYING THAT YOU WOULD PROBABLY BE HERE ALL SUMMER

Copyright, 1924, by The Bell Syndicate, Inc.

YOU KNOW ME AL   That's Taking Advantage of the Other Guy   —By RING W. LARDNER

WHY DON'T YOU WRITE A SONG AND CLEAN UP A BUNCH OF MONEY?

WHAT ARE YOU TALKIN' ABOUT. A BASEBALL PITCHER WRITIN' SONGS?

WHY THIS CLUB USED TO HAVE A LEFT-HAND PITCHER NAMED DOC WHITE AND HE WROTE A SONG, "LITTLE PUFF OF SMOKE." I HEARD IT ON THE RADIO LAST WINTER FROM STATION WFAA, DALLAS

WELL, I GUESS I COULD WRITE ONE IF A LEFT-HANDER COULD? BUT WHAT WOULD I WRITE ONE ABOUT AND WHAT WOULD I CALL IT?

WHY, WRITE A SONG ABOUT BASEBALL AND CALL IT, "TAKE ME OUT TO THE BALL GAME."

BUT IT SEEMS TO ME LIKE I'VE ALREADY HEARD A SONG CALLED, TAKE ME OUT TO THE BALL GAME. PRETTY GOOD SONG, TOO ... !

ALL THE MORE REASON WHY YOU SHOULD GIVE YOUR SONG THAT NAME

PEOPLE'LL BUY YOUR SONG THINKIN' IT'S THE GOOD ONE

Copyright, 1924, by The Bell Syndicate, Inc.   3-10-24

110

Friend Al:

Well Al I am waiting for Joe Whelan to help me make out my income tax and you want to be thankful Al that you dont make no big money as the govt. takes it all away from you as fast as you make it and what do you think of a man Al who my salery aint only $2500.00 dollars per annum and I have got to pay a tax of pretty near $1300.00 on acct. of $17000.00 I cleaned up with Whelan in that oil least. I was not going to menshun it but Whelan says the people who bought the least off us will report it to the govt. and if I had of known what kind of tattle tales they was I would not of had no dealings with them money or no money. The oil business is a great business to stay away from which I guest some of our high mucky mucks is finding that out every day.

Jack Keefe

Friend Al:

Well Al today we play the N.Y. giants and tomorrow the St. Louis nationals and after that we have got a game pretty near every day with some national league club and I bet by the time we get threw with them they will be thanking there stars that they dont half to hit vs. our kind of pitching all the yr. around or they would half to send a tracer after there batting average. I hope I will get a chance to pitch vs. this here Hornsby who all the other clubs is trying to buy him for a 1-2 a million dollars and if they happen to have there scouts on the ground when I pitch vs. him why they will change there offer to a 1-2 a dozen used whiskers.

Jack Keefe

Friend Al:

It begins to look like I wont be a White Sox much longer Al thanks heavens and the blow off cant come to soon to suit me as a man cant get a square deal on this club and I cant do my best work when I know some of the other boys is pulling vs. me. It is just a question of jellus and somebody another has been telling Evers I aint trying. Well Al I dont half to tell you that I always try but even did I not try I can out pitch anybody on this club when they are trying. Any way theys no chance of me getting out of this league Al as they couldent never get wafers so I will go to what club makes the best offer and all as I hope is that it will be some club that has got a chance for the old pennant as I am sick in tired of pitching for a club that thinks one game in a row is a winning streek.

Jack Keefe

(Copyright, 1924, by The Bell Syndicate, Inc.)

Friend Al:

Well Al dont be supprised if you here that your old pal is traded to the Yankees. One of the boys got a hold of a N.Y. paper today and it says in it that Mgr. Huggins was trying to pull off a deal with our club and did not say who he was going to give up but says he was libel to get a young pitcher and a infielder. Well Al the only young pitcher who they could reffer to is myself as we aint got no other young pitcher who Huggins would look at unlest he wanted a good laugh. I guest that would be tough luck to get traded off this club to a club that cant hardly help from win the pennant a specially when they have got me and live in the big town besides where a man gets apresiated. Oh you gray white way.

Jack Keefe

(Copyright, 1924, by The Bell Syndicate, Inc.)

Friend Al:

Well Al I suppose by this time you seen in the paper where your old pal has became a member of the worlds champs. The news come last night that I and Joe Whelan had been traded to the Yankees for a man name Gates who none of the boys seems to know much about him but he must be pretty good or this club would not of never left me go. I am tickled to death that old Joe is going along with me as we are great pals but of coarse he was just throwed in on acct. of this club not haveing no use for him. Well Al the Yanks looked pretty good before but this makes them a cinch and you must come down to N.Y. next fall and see your old pal pitch a worlds serious game and I would not be supprised if Huggins use me in the 1st. game so as he will be sure of haveing me ready for another game if nessary. I and Joe leaves here tonight and will join the Yanks at Columbus, Geo. wear they have got a exhibition. I bet Ruth and the rest of them will give 3 cheers when they see us blow in.

                      Jack Keefe

Friend Al:

Well Al 1 of the other marred men on the N.Y. club has just been telling me that I would be a sucker to move my Mrs. from Chi to N.Y. as I had told him that we got a 5 rm. apt. in Chi. for $175.00 per mo. which he says you cant even rent a phone booth in N.Y. for that amt. of money and the way he does it is leave his Mrs. at there home in Ft. Wayne dureing the baseball season and he rents a rm. in N.Y. and then she pays him a visit along in July or August. So I have wrote Edna to stay in Chi. till we make our 1st. westren trip and then we can talk it over and mean wile we can live cheper apart and if the Yanks wins another penant and world serious like it looks like they cant help doing now they have got me, why we can say to he--ll with expences and next fall we can take a long least on the swellest apt. on 6 ave.

Jack Keefe

Friend Al:

Well Al we hit the big town tomorrow and play a game with the Brooklyn club at the stadum and some of the boys has warned me that I wont have no time to warm up or nothing else because all the N.Y. newspaper boys will be wanting to take my picture so I says in a jokeing way that I better disguise myself when I show up on the field and ware a falts beard or something and maybe they will leave me alone. So Charley O'Leary the coach says you dont half to ware a falts beard to disguise yourself, just get out there and pitch a good game of ball and they wont nobody beleive its you. He is a great kidder Al and we been kidding back and 4th. ever since I jointed the club and I guest you know who got the best of it but you cant help from likeing him if you take him the right way. But jokeing to 1 side I am a friend of the newspaper boys and if they want to take my picture they are wellcome provide it they dont keep pesting me when I am getting ready to work.

Jack Keefe

Dear Al:

Well Al here it is opening day and did not think it would never come and was never so anxius in my life to get started as am sure with a winner this yr. and all as I hope is that Huggins will leave me pitch this P.M. so I can show him I am right and then he will use me in my regular term. All as I half to do with this Boston club is make a face at them and they are licked and I told that to Charley O'Leary and he says then I could beat them without no effort at all. Must clothes now as O'Leary is becking to me and maybe has got a message from Huggins that I am going to pitch.

Jack Keefe

Friend Al:

Well Al just got back to the big town and now we stay here till we make our 1st westren trip so it looks like we should ought to have a home so Edna has picked out a cottage out near Rye which you can go swimming in L.I. sound but she is braging about haveing 3 bath rooms in the cottage which I dont see what you want of 1 bath room if you got a hole sound to swim in let alone 3 but that is the woman for you. I am all threw argueing with them Al so I am going to leave her sine the least and she says she is getting the best of it because it is a furnish cottage and we dont half to buy no furniture. I suppose I should ought to thank heavens that she aint rented Central Pk. for a year and guaranteed to upholster it.

Jack Keefe

YOU KNOW ME AL   By Ring Lardner

Friend Al:

Well Al I ast Edna yesterday how she come to pick Rye for a place to live and she says so as her sister could come in contract with smart people so I says why dident we pick somewheres in New Jersey and maybe she could come in contract with Thos. M. Edison. As for Rye being so smart we stayed in N.Y. to a show last night and come out on the last train and I set in the smoker and I guest I was about the only man liveing in Rye that the conductor did not half to wake them up and tell them it was there station. From the looks of the rest of the boys about the only smart thing they ever done was name the town and they might as well of called it scotch.

Jack Keefe

Friend Al:

Well Al what do you think, my old pals the White Sox is here and Huggins has promised to pitch me vs. them to morrow and it will be my 1st. start and I guess I wont make a monkey out of them and they will see what a sucker they was to leave me go. It is a set up for me Al as I know them like a book and all there weakness and they will be lucky to score let alone any chance they got of wining. I been wandering what Huggins was saveing me for but now I know and I am tickled to death he aint over worked me so I will be in my best condition which I guest I dont half to tell you what that means.

Jack Keefe

(Copyright. 1924, by The Bell Syndicate, Inc.)

YOU KNOW ME AL   By Ring Lardner

Friend Al:

Well Al Edna is tickled to death because some of the women has ast her to join a kind of a club which they meet once a wk. and disgust tropics of the day and politics and etc. and she says besides giveing her a chance to meet the smart set around Rye why it will also keep her mind on edge and I dont know what she wants it on edge for as it dont look to me like she was ever going to use it or no other woman. But I aint got no objections and she can join all the clubs she feels like as long as it dont cost nothing and at lease it will keep her away from N. Y. one day per wk. which so far she has acted like she was the janitor of 5th. ave. and was suppose to open it mornings and close it nights.

Jack Keefe

(Copyright, 1924, by The Bell Syndicate, Inc.)

Friend Al:

Well Al I guest I showed them something in there today and beat Cleveland 4 to 1 and they would not of had that 1 only for the wind blowing a ball fair which Burns hit which would of been 10 ft. foul only for the wind and at that it looked like a foul ball to me but the empires in this league says the 1st. thing that come in to there head. But I certainly had the boys biteing out of my hand and even Speaker paid me a complement and I walked past him in the 7th. innings and I says how do I look in there today Spoke and he says I cant beleive its you. They call him Spoke on acct. of his name being Speaker.

Jack Keefe

Friend Al:

Well Al today is the last game of the Detroit serious and I am going to ask Huggins to leave me pitch as this is one club I have got there goat and they are licked the minute I begin to warm up. The good hitting clubs is easy for me Al as I always pitch my best vs. them where as when I work vs. a club that cant hit very good I genally always feel sorry for them and ease up. A man should not ought to leave sympathy effect there ball playing but I cant help the way I was made and I would rather loose a game once in a wile than be the cause of some ball player loosing there job when they maybe got wifes and kiddies to sport.

Jack Keefe

Friend Al:

    I pitched vs. my old team mates the White Sox today and certianly give them a triming and made a monkey out of them and beat them 3 to 2 in 10 inning because the boys could not hit behind me or would of licked them in 9 inning. In the 1 inning I was not warmed up very good and give 2 base on balls and this here Sheely hit a 3 base hit which I was trying to waist one on bim and at that the ball he hit was a foul but talking to 1 of these empires is like making a speech to a brick wall and I know there names is Rowland and Dinneen and Connolly and etc. but if you don't call them something stronger they wont pay no tension. Finely they was a couple of the boys got on and the Babe hit one right over 2d. base and I suppose they would of called that a foul only they couldent find a archtest to change the field. Well anyways I win and tomorrow we go to St. Louis and if Huggins will jest leave me pitch why this here Sisler will of wisht he had of stayed out of baseball another yr.

Jack Keefe

Friend Al:

Well I guest you seen what I done agin Detroit yesterday and for once I got a sqare deal from the empires and had the boys eating out of my hand. They call them the Tigers Al but by the time I got threw with them there right name was house cats. Heilman only hit 2 out of the infield and all as Cobb could get off of me was a base on balls a scratch double and single and I had him struck out the 1st. time he come up but I was trying to curve one and the ball sliped and did not break so he got a hold of it. Any way I beat them 6 and 5 and Cobb was so sore he called me lucky and tried to start a argument but I guest he wont try it again after what I told him.

Jack Keefe

Friend Al:

Well Al here we are in Cleveland where they had the big convention last wk. and 1 of the Cleveland reporters was a round to our hotel last night and I ast him was it true that the delegates had sqawked because Boston was schedule here instead of we and he says they was a hole lot of them out to the games holling for the Babe and I and on acct. of we not being here they voted to not hold no more natl. conventions here for another yr. at the outside. Some of these men had came all the way from Denver and Colorado and probly the only chance they ever had to see real baseball stars in actions and look at the treatmunt they give them. Of course the Boston club has did pretty good so far this yr. but after all they aint us.

Jack Keefe

Friend Al:

Landed home today off our westren trip expecting maybe Edna would be glad to see me but she was out somewheres with her sister and when I opened up the front door why instead of she giveing me a wellcome why a great big german police dog give a running jump at me and tried to kiss me with his mouth wide open. I throwed my suit case at him and managed to get the door shut with me outside and set there on the porch till Edna and Lottie finely come home and we went in together and he jumped at us all but she says he was just playing. I guest Dempsey was just playing with Firpo, any way it seems wile I was away she bought him off a guy for $100.00 as he told her it was a big bargun as the dog just got here from germany and as far as I am conserned I will give another $100.00 if he will take the next boat back. That is the he--ll of it in baseball Al it costs to much to take your wife on a trip and it aint safe to leave them home.

Jack Keefe

Friend Al:

This is the wk. of the democrat convention here in N.Y. and this time theys a treat in store for the delegates as we are schedule for 3 days with the Washington club and you could not ask for a better lay out hey Al with the champions of the world playing vs. the capital. I would not be supprised if Huggins would pitch me today as the convention opens up tomorrow and after it starts the delegates may be to busy to come out to the games. They will be a sore bunch if they dont get a look at the Babe and I wile they are here though I guest the Washington club will be tickeled to death if I stay on the bench but we aint running our ball club to please them hey Al.

Jack Keefe

Friend Al:

Well Al some of the boys that has been trying to kid me has got the shoe on the other ft. this time and I guest they wont kid me no more after what I done to the Washington club yesterday with Johnson pitching and beat them 5 and 1 and would of shet them out only for the empires giveing Judge a 3 base hit in the 8th. innings when the ball was so far foul that the boys in the press box ducked there heads. After the game I says to Huggins well what do you think of me now and he says I think just the same like I have always thought some times your good and some times your rotten. You look like the best pitcher in the league when you aint the worst so you see what he thinks of me Al and from now it looks like he would work me in my regular term.

Jack Keefe

Friend Al:

Well Al some of the boys on the club was saying how the Washington club had about shot there bold and here for a wile it looked like Walter Johnson was finely going to get a chance to pitch in a world serious but now it looks like they are threw and Charley O'Leary said it was tough that a man like Johnson could not never show what he could do in a big serious like that and how the public would be dissapoint it on acct. of not being able to see Johnson in a big serious. But he said of coarse if Washington had of win the pennant why the public would also be dissapoint it on acct. of not seen what Jack Keefe could do in a world serious, so Joe Whelan says why we all ready know what Jack would do in a world serious, he would watch it very carefull. So I says is that so. Joe may be a great kidder but he cant kid me.

Jack Keefe

Friend Al:

Well Al we got word from the bank today that Edna had overdrawed her acct. $35.00 and she says they must be some mistake so I overlooked her check book and I wished you could see the way she has been throwing money a round and it is a wonder she aint overdrawed $3500.00 let alone $35.00. They was 1 check for $80.00 made out to some stables and I ast her what was that and it seems her and her sister has been lerning to ride horse back and I suppose they want to be all set in case the Prince of Wales calls them up when he gets over here and they was another check for $65.00 for flowers which she says she had her bridge club here one P.M. and had to have flowers on the table and I guest they must been diamond studded orchards from the price of them. When I was in the Central League Al and makeing $125.00 per mo. I had plenty money to spend and nothing to worry about and now I am with the champions of the world and it looks like my next step up will be in to the poor house.

Jack Keefe

(Copyright, 1924, by The Bell Syndicate, Inc.)

The Busher Abroad

Friend Al:

Well Al I bet this will be a big surprrise to you, we are going to europe and France just I and Edna. Our least on our house here in Rye is up the 15 of Oct. and we aint got no other home and Edna pointed out where it would be just as cheap for us to take a trip a broad and see something as try and live a round here. It certainly will be grand Al to be sailing acrost the old pond and see the sites and will drop you a post card once and a wile and leave you know where we are. We are going to sale on the steamer Paris and on the french line, it is named after the town of Paris. Well Al havent no time to write much but bond voyage and will drop you a post card once and a wile.

Jack Keefe

Friend Al:

Well Al I am writeing this on the bord of the steamer Paris and I wished you was along. She is a great big boat Al and bigger then the boats that run between Chicago and Benton Harbor. She would half to be as the waves is higher then lake Michigan. I and Edna has got a rm. with a private bath rm. only you feel worst after you get threw with a bath then before you had it as the soap wont leather and the salt water sticks to a person. Just think Al in about a wk. we will be in gay Paris. Oh you gay Paris.

Jack Keefe

131

Friend Al:

Well Al we are 1/2 way across the old pond and only 3 days more and we will be in old France. I been kind of keeping to my state rm. and laying low as I dont want nobody to know who I am or they would be pesting the life out of me. I come over here to get a rest and get a way from the fans and admires. So when ever I go up on 1 of the decks I kind of pull my cap down over my face so they wont nobody reckonize me. When a person like I comes on a trip like this kind you have got to keep a way from people or they wont give you no piece.

Jack Keefe

Friend Al:

Well Al we landed last night in France in a town called Harvey which they say it means the harbor and I dont see why they cant come right out and call it harbor and be done with it. One of the men on the boat says it was the custom to open up our baggage and see what was in it and Edna says it was none of there business and she did not want nobody prying into our affairs so I told him if I catched any body opening up our baggage I would bust them in the jaw. All he could answer back was mumble something in French. They took our trunk off of the ship last night but I guest they did not try no monkey business as we had it locked up and a couple straps tied a round it. I am still on the bord of the ship waiting for time for the old rattler to start for Paris which we will get there about noon. Oh you gay Paris

Jack Keefe

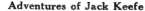

Friend Al:

Well Al we been in gay Paris a couple days now and it certainly is some berg and if a person was not marred and had there wife along you could certainly have a lot of excitement as every gal you see acts like they want to get acquainted. Edna dont want to do nothing only buy close as she says this is where all the swell woman in America buys there close but all the prices is in francs which one day they are so much and the next day some other amt. and they wont tell you how much they are going to be the next day so you dont know when to buy. Tonight we are going to a show called the follies Berger which they tell me is some live show.

Jack Keefe

Friend Al:

They talk about haveing prohibition in America and how tough it is but here in Paris you cant even get water to say nothing about matches. So far it looks to me like gay Paris was a town where your wife spends a couple 100 dollars on a dress which you could get same in N. Y. for one 100 dollars but they want to show a Paris labble. Persoaly I aint boughten nothing over here only cigarettes and if you can get threw the first package you might live a yr. but otherwise you are sunk. In regards to the beer, you might order beer or mable syrup and you get the same thing.

Jack Keefe

Friend

Well Al we been here in Paris over a wk. now and they tell me that back in 1914 the Germans tried to take Paris but I dont know what for and as far as I am concerned who ever takes it can keep it. I would certainly hate to live in a town where they talk as fast like they do here and expect you to understand what and the he—ll are they talking about and you talk back to them slow and they dont know what and the he—ll are you saying. When you just call them dumb-bells you are giveing them a big boost.

Jack Keefe

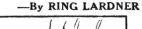

Friend Al:

Paris has certainly got a great bunch of traffic cops Al, they either pick out the corners where they aint no traffic or else they stand on the busy corners and act blind like some of the empires in our league. If a man rides 3 blocks in a taxi in this town and dont loose a leg or something why its a merkle. And the worst of it is that if you dont ride in a taxi you half to walk and then you aint got no chance at all. I and Edna seen a man flying over the town this A.M. in a air plain and Edna says how much nerve he must have but beleif me he was the safest man in Paris.

Jack Keefe

Friend Al:

Well Al when we come over here I give Edna $500.00 which she says would be all she would spend all the time we are in Europe and now we aint only been in Paris about 10 days and this A.M. she was borring 2 franks to buy stamps for some post cards to send home. And all she has boughten is some foney pearls and a couple party dresses which all as she can do with them is dress up and look in the glass as we dont never get invited to no parties when wear home. But the minute a woman gets to Paris they go crazy on the subject of close though the women that lives here looks like they had not boughten nothing new since the French resolutions.

Jack Keefe

Friend Al:

Well Al I been hearing all my life about French cooking and how tasty it is and etc. but I aint found no place in Paris yet where you can get food that tastes like anything and I been keeping my arm in shape shakeing salt which you could eat a bbl. of it and not even make you thirsty. And if you did get thirsty you would be out of luck as they aint no waiter in France that ever heard of a drink of water.

Jack Keefe

Friend Al:

Well Al I dont know nothing about history only what I lerned in school but I always thought that France was a country long before the old U.S. was ever heard of and yet the way they run things over here in Paris why you would think this country was about 1yr. old and the U.S. had been going along sense the garden of Edom. Like for inst. you dont get no soap in the hotels here unless you ask for it and then you half to ask them for du savon when soap aint nowheres near as hard to say.

Jack Keefe

"YOU KNOW ME AL."   The Adventures of Jack Keefe.   By Ring Lardner.

Friend Al:

Well Al it looks like we would be starting back to the old U.S.A. as soon as we can get a boat. I been willing to go home ever since we got to Paris but did not want to spoil Edna's pleasure but last night she begin hinting like she was about threw enjoin her self so I says how about going home and she says I am for it. The truth is Al that she cant get along without no women to talk to and she cant talk this here French and in the 2nd place she has boughten a whole lot of fancy close and she wants to get back and show them off and tell where she got them. Any ways I am tickeld to death and the sooner we can get home why I am tickeld to death.

Jack Keefe

Friend Al:

Well Al here we are on the old pond again bound for the old U. S. and arrive in old N. Y. some time Saturday. Will go to hotel till we make up our mind where wear going to live this winter. Edna wants to live in N. Y. so as she can throw money away faster. Personly I dont care as long as its in the old U. S. as I am threw with farm countrys and all the rideing I will do after this will be in a taxi or on a train. Dont never leave nobody talk you into a trip a broad Al though I guest they aint no danger as it certainly costs a hole lot of money.

Jack Keefe

Friend Al:

Well Al only 3 more days and we will be getting off of the Paris and the rest of the trip aint going to be as tiresome like the 1st. part as I got aquainted today with a couple of Americans that want me to play cards with them tonight and tomorrow. They are from Boston and seen me pitch vs. the Boston club and was crazy to meet me and one of them says he wished the Boston club would trade Ehmke for myself so it looks like they are pretty clean cut high class boys and not dum bells like the most of the people on the ship.

Jack Keefe

The Busher Plays Sleuth

Friend Al:

Well we been back in N. Y. 3 days now and stopping at this hotel and I keep telling Edna to hurry up and find us a apartment or something but she says what is the hurry as we are pretty comftible where we are so I says we wont be so comftible when the bill comes a round at the end of the wk. Wear paying $6.00 per day Al for a little dinky rm. which I suppose is more then you make in a wk. and that dont include meals. It is costing us about $15.00 per day to live as Edna eats like a horse and I aint making nothing per day so where wear going to head in at is a misery to me.

Jack Keefe

144

Friend Al:

Well Al I been worring all wk. on acct. of not haveing no job and it is costing us a bbl. of money to live but I guest my worrys is over. I met a man in the hotel this A. M. t at is in Wall st. where all the high mucky mucks sells stocks and they make a bbl. of money and he says why dont you tackle the game and I says I would think it over and he says the only way to do is buy a seat on the stock exchange and go at it right. So tomorrow I am going down and buy a seat and look them over and if I like the game I will go to it. You can bet they wont put nothing over on me Al as I aint no sucker where big money is conserned and dont be supprised if you hear about me going in partners with Morgan hey Al.

Jack Keefe

145

Friend Al:

Well Al here I am in the biggest city in the world and you would think it would be easy for a man like I to land a good position of some kind another but so far the best offer I had was $15.00 per wk. and that wouldent even pay Ednas barber bill. A fellow was telling me yesterday that theys a swell new mens store on 5th. ave. where they have men models with fine physics to show off the suits and coats and etc. Well Al I dident never think I would fall low enought to be a model but it begins to look like I couldent be choosey and I am going down and see them today and I guest when they see how I am built they will hire me without even asking me how much do I want.

Jack Keefe

Friend Al:

Well Al I finely landed a good job and go to work tomorrow A.M. and the job is collector for Hyde and Bowman a great big furniture store that sells on the easy payment plan, that is the people dont pay for there furniture when they get it but pays so much per wk. and when they get behind in there payments it is up to me to go to there house and get the amt. they are behind. This will be a cinch Al as it will keep me out in the open air and I should ought to clean up a bbl. of money as they are going to pay me 50 per cent of all I collect besides a big fat salery.

Jack Keefe.

149

Friend Al:

Well Al I have give up my job with Hyde and Bowman as I aint cold blood it enough for a collector a specially when its poor people you half to collect from. I was on the job 2 days and then I told Mr. Hyde the boss that I could not work for them no more as I was not mean enough for that kind of a job. He says well Keefe we are sorry to loose you and wished you would reconsider but I said no Mr. Hyde I would-ent never be happy in a position where I was makeing others suffer. So we shook hands and he payed me off and now I got to look for another job but you can bet it wont be no collector job which I got to big a heart for that kind of business.

                                  Jack Keefe.

Friend Al:

Well Al only 3 days till xmas and what a fine xmas it will be for Edna and I without hardily any money and no home you might say and no friends to invite us to there house. Well one thing I wont half to puzzle my brains about what presents to get for different people as I aint got nothing to buy presents with and that reminds me Al that I wont be able to send you a tie this xmas like usual and the tie I sent you last xmas will half to do you another yr. and I hope it aint all wore out though I dont suppose it is as you dont very often wear a tie. Any way Mary xmas to you and Bertha and it is a cinch you will at lease have as Mary a xmas as your pal

Jack Keefe.

Friend Al:

Well Al I finely got a job that suits me to a T, 2 days ago a fella from the N. Y. Central offered me a job as R.R. detective and you know me Al I dident want to be no cinder dick so past it up. This morning I fell into what I calls a soft snap. 1 of the big hotels here advertized for a house detective and I got it. I am now a house dick and dont do nothing but look for crooks and sharpers round the lobby for which I grabs off a pretty big salery and have free ontray to the dining rm. That last feed bag item is a pick up eh Al. Well I got to polish up my badge now

          yours in haist
             Jack Keefe

Friend Al:

Well Al Im on my first big job now. Most hotel lobbys is full of sharpers that is always robbing out of town guests. My job now is to sit around in disguise and grab the 1st smart alek that tries to handle me. Im going to look stupid and sit and wait. Right now the hotel is a big rat trap all set and ready to spring and the peace of chese is no other than

          Your friend
             Jack Keefe

Friend Al:

The tailor that has a store on the ground floor of the hotel here says that pickpockets bother the crowds looking in his winders and he wants to have a few of them caught. Knowing that I have got a eye like the well known eegle he asked the boss to have me play the part of the dummy in the winder and wile so doing that I should ought to keep my eye out for the dips.

So Al this morning Ill be dressed up with a sine on me reading take me home for $23.98 and so 4th. And Al think how still I have to stand. Imitation wood is some job for a man but nobody will try harder than

your pal
Jack Keefe

Friend Al:

Well Al I almost shocked that fat guy in rm 79 to death this morning. You know Al I meet all sorts of people here and pick up language fast. This wk. I spoke to frenchmen englishmen turks and hindoos. I know a gag in every language. Well Al this morning that fat guy past me and says with a snicker bon jour monsewer. I smiled and came right back with mayonaisse cafe parfay. Well Al he almost fell over in a feint he was so surprized at my edjucation. Then I smiled and says you aint talking to nobody thats dumb you know. Im no sap Al you know I didnt spend two wks on the rue della pay for nothing.

Well buy buy Al more later

Jack Keefe.

Friend Al:

Well Al things aint changed any around this joint. Im still on the job and getting smarted up all the time by wise people which I meet in the lobby and other parts of the hotel. Today I had a nice talk with a college guy which is stopping here for awile. He was talking about the language used by people now adays which aint got no class at all and I agrees with him when he says a mans got to stop and think to find out what the other guy is talking about. Like for instance our baggidge man has got a line all his own which is different from the elevator boys and so 4th and so 4th. Im afraid that when I gets home again my missus wont know nothing that Im saying Im getting so smarted up.

Jack Keefe.

On January 9, 1925, Ring Lardner wrote to F. Scott Fitzgerald: "I have quit the strip and Dick Dorgan is doing it with help from Tad." Lardner had apparently worked about a month ahead. Though "You Know Me Al" continued to carry his name until September 26, 1925, it is virtually certain that he had no hand in strips that appeared after mid-February of that year.

A Guide to the Players

Nick Altrock: Pitcher who joined the Washington Senators in 1912 but pitched only eighteen games in seven seasons as an active player for Washington. His job was to entertain the crowd with antics on the field.

Benny Bengough: Relief catcher for the New York Yankees from 1923 to 1930.

Mordecai "Three-Finger" Brown: Pitcher from 1903 to 1916, primarily with the Chicago Cubs. His lifetime won-lost record was 239–135.

Frank Chance: Played for the Chicago Cubs from 1898 to 1912. First baseman in the famous double-play combination Tinker to Evers to Chance. Chance was briefly manager of the Chicago White Sox in spring 1924 before being replaced by Johnny Evers.

Ty Cobb: Outfielder for the Detroit Tigers from 1905 to 1926. Among his all-time records are career hits (4,191), career batting average (.367), and career runs (2,244).

Charles A. Comiskey: Founder of the Chicago White Sox in 1900 and owner of the team until his death in 1931. With Ban Johnson, Comiskey started the American League, also in 1900. In 1923 he was one of the most powerful men in baseball.

Thomas H. Connolly: American League umpire, 1901–1937.

William H. Dinneen: American League umpire, 1909–1937.

Howard Ehmke: Pitcher from 1915 to 1930 for various American League teams, including the Boston Red Sox from 1923 to 1925. His won-lost record in 1924 was 19–17.

Johnny Evers: Second baseman in the famous Chicago Cubs double-play combination Tinker to Evers to Chance. Evers managed the Chicago White Sox for one year, 1924.

William J. "Kid" Gleason: Manager of the Chicago White Sox from 1919 to 1923.

Clark Griffith: Manager of the Washington Senators from 1912 to 1920; owner from 1921 until his death in 1951. He managed the Senators when Nick Altrock first came to the team.

Harry Hooper: Outfielder for the Boston Red Sox from 1909 to 1920 and for the Chicago White Sox from 1921 to 1925.

Miller Huggins: Manager of the New York Yankees from 1918 to 1929. During that time his team won the pennant six times and the World Series three times, including 1923.

Hugh "Ee-Yah" Jennings: Manager of the Detroit Tigers from 1907 to 1920; coach for the New York Giants in the twenties. Jennings was known for his vocal encouragement of his players.

Walter "The Big Train" Johnson: Pitcher for the Washington Senators from 1907 to 1927. He holds the all-time records for most shut-outs (113) and most career strikeouts (3,503).

Joe Judge: First baseman for the Washington Senators from 1915 to 1932. In 1924 his batting average was .324.

Ed "Strangler" Lewis: Heavyweight wrestling champion from 1920 to 1932, during the days when professional wrestling was a legitimate sport.

Harvey McClellan: Infielder for the Chicago White Sox from 1919 to 1924. The only year McClellan was a starter for a full season was 1923.

Connie Mack: Known as "The Tall Tactician," Mack managed the Philadelphia Athletics from 1901 to 1950. Philadelphia finished seventh in the American League in 1922, sixth in 1923. Mack also managed the franchise for the Athletics and by 1940 owned 50 percent of the team.

Christy "Big Six" Mathewson: Pitcher for the New York Giants from 1900 to 1916. Mathewson's career won-lost record is 373–188; his best-known pitch was the "fade-away" ball.

Johnny Mostil: Outfielder for the Chicago White Sox from 1918 to 1929.

Charley O'Leary: Shortstop for the Detroit Tigers from 1904 to 1912. From 1920 to 1930 he was coach of the New York Yankees and was considered instrumental in the Yankee domination of the American League in the twenties.

Clarence Rowland: American League umpire, 1923–1927.

Colonel Jacob Ruppert: Owner of the New York Yankees from 1915 until his death in 1939. Though his business interests centered around his Ruppert Brewing Company, Ruppert's avocation was baseball. As owner of the Yankees, Ruppert bought Babe Ruth from the Boston Red Sox, built Yankee Stadium, and won ten pennants and seven World Series championships.

Babe Ruth: Traded from the Boston Red Sox to the New York Yankees in 1920, Ruth led the American League in home runs in all but two years between 1918 and 1930—with eleven in 1918, twenty-nine in 1919, fifty-four in 1920, and fifty-nine in 1921.

Ray Schalk: Catcher for the Chicago White Sox from 1912 to 1928. He was second in all-time career assists for a catcher (1,811).

Joe Sewell: Shortstop and later third baseman for the Cleveland Indians from 1920 to 1930. In 1923 his batting average was .353.

Earl "Whitey" Sheeley: Chicago White Sox first baseman from 1921 to 1927. His batting average in 1924 was .320.

Tris Speaker: Outfielder from 1907 to 1928; played for the Cleveland Indians from 1916 to 1926. He led the league in doubles (59) and RBIs (130) in 1923 and had a .380 batting average that year.

Amos Alonzo Stagg: Football coach at the University of Chicago from 1892 to 1933; there he won 268 games and lost 141 while originating many principles of modern play.

Ed Walsh: Pitcher, primarily for the Chicago White Sox, from 1904 to 1917. He had the all-time lowest career ERA (1.82).

G. Harris "Doc" White: Pitcher for the Chicago White Sox from 1903 to 1913. White wrote the music for two songs with lyrics by Lardner: "Little Puff of Smoke Good Night" (1910) and "Gee! It's a Wonderful Game" (1911).

Ross Youngs: Outfielder for the New York Giants from 1917 to 1926. He hit .331 in 1922 and .336 in 1923.

Afterword

Ring Lardner was not the first noted American author to adapt his prose to a nationally syndicated comic strip format. As early as August 28, 1904, the *Chicago Record-Herald* introduced a Sunday color page called "Queer Visitors from the Marvellous Land of Oz," with art by the then-famed Walt McDougall and original text by L. Frank Baum, which developed further escapades of Baum's *Wizard of Oz* characters. A decade or so later, Gelette Burgess drew his "Goops" into a *Chicago Tribune* Sunday strip, and Will Rogers launched a daily strip in October 1920 called "Will Rogers (Himself) in What's News Today," with "Drawings by Roy Grove" and "Jokes by Will Rogers." Such strips proliferated in the 1920s, from J. P. McEvoy's adaptation of his hit play *The Potters* in 1923 to Octavus Roy Cohen's all-black-character reworking of his *Saturday Evening Post* stories in "Tempus Todd" the same year. An early entry in this spate of prose-adapted strips was Ring Lardner's "You Know Me Al," first published in September 1922; it was also one of the most popular and longest running of such works. In fact, only three fiction-derived strips ever exceeded "Al" in circulation: Edgar Rice Burroughs's "Tarzan," Dashiell Hammett's "Secret Agent X-9," and Peter B. Kyne's "Cappy Ricks," all introduced in the 1930s.

Many newspapers, notably the morning papers of the Hearst chain, chose to run "Al" on the sports page. Although there had been many famed sports page strips since Bud Fisher's 1907 "A. Mutt" (later "Mutt and Jeff"), such as Billy De Beck's "Barney Google," Frank Willard's early "Moon Mullins," Ken Kling's "Joe and Asbestos,"

Ham Fisher's "Joe Palooka," and Tad Dorgan's "Silk-Hat Harry" and "Judge Rummy" series, most such strips centered on horse racing or boxing. Baseball-oriented strips were comparatively uncommon; Don Armstrong's forgotten "Bill Bull" in the 1913 daily *Chicago Tribune* and Russ Westover's amusing *San Francisco Post* series of the 1910s—"Daffy Dan," "Baseball Bugs," and "Luke McGluck"—were among the earliest.

Lardner's association with comic art did not begin with "Al." Eight years earlier he had enjoyed a close relationship with one of the most talented cartoonists of all time. Prior to Fontaine Fox's swift ascension to fame with his "Toonerville Folks" daily panel and Sunday page after the end of World War I, he illustrated a series of Lardner stories and sketches in *Redbook* between 1914 and 1918, some of which later appeared in Lardner's *Own Your Own Home* (1919). Fox also drew a number of original vignettes for a collection of Lardner's comic poetry, *Bib Ballads* (1915). Lardner also relished a friendly sports-page feud with Sidney Smith of "The Gumps" before that strip left the pages of the *Chicago Tribune* to enter upon the national syndication it later enjoyed. Smith's daily "Gumps" usually ran just a few inches away from Lardner's daily column, "In the Wake of the News," and from 1916 to 1918 friendly insults were exchanged regularly between the two. Lardner made fun of cartooning in general, while Smith portrayed Lardner as a neighbor of the Gumps who made a pest of himself by borrowing things he never returned. (Smith and Lardner were, in fact, near neighbors in a Chicago suburb at the time.) When Lardner quit the *Chicago Tribune* to write for the Bell Syndicate, a comic strip version of his most successful series of stories, "The Busher's Letters," was a natural development.

Of the two cartoonists who worked with Lardner on "Al," Will B. Johnstone was somewhat better known at the time. A magazine and book illustrator in the comic vein prior to "Al," Johnstone was later noted for his political cartoons for the *New York World,* of which the best known was probably the tribute to Sir Arthur Conan Doyle (and Sherlock Holmes), published at the time of Doyle's death in 1930. Clearly not a cartoonist of natural talent or quick visual appeal, Johnstone was generally obscure during his life and would be forgotten today if it were not for his association with Lardner in "Al." Much the same is true of Dick Dorgan, whose only other claim to any kind of derived fame is the fact that he was the brother of the very great Tad Dorgan—a fact that plainly obtained him the few newspaper syndicate jobs he held. A trace of his brother's famed adeptness with vernacular English is perceptible in Dick Dorgan's "Kid Dugan," a boxing strip of the mid-1920s which he developed out of "Al" when Lardner left the strip. But the art is secondary; Lardner's inimitable prose and the attractiveness of his classic numbskull Jack Keefe clearly constitute the major part of the show in "Al."

—Bill Blackbeard